A TEMPTING DILEMMA

"So you had a happy childhood."

"I did."

Philip stared into the distance. "I was in constant trouble. Everything my older brothers did was blamed on me."

"And if you started in the navy at age twelve, your actual childhood was rather short."

"Not too short for me to believe what everyone thought of me. I enjoyed being a demon."

"So why are you surprised that your half sister is such a handful?"

"Touché! Miss Elliott, you are indeed perceptive."

"Oh, just observant, I think."

They laughed at the same time. Rosalind turned toward him and their eyes met. The laughter faded and they sat still, the moment lengthening. Rosalind felt sure he could hear the pounding of her heart.

Her heart raced out of control at the thought he might kiss her. The tension between them grew stronger, like the lull just before a great storm breaks. She wanted to lose herself in the gale, wanted it to sweep over her, wanted to drown in his arms. . . .

BOOK YOUR PLACE ON OUR WEBSITE AND MAKE THE READING CONNECTION!

We've created a customized website just for our very special readers, where you can get the inside scoop on everything that's going on with Zebra, Pinnacle and Kensington books.

When you come online, you'll have the exciting opportunity to:

- View covers of upcoming books
- Read sample chapters
- Learn about our future publishing schedule (listed by publication month *and author*)
- Find out when your favorite authors will be visiting a city near you
- Search for and order backlist books from our online catalog
- Check out author bios and background information
- Send e-mail to your favorite authors
- Meet the Kensington staff online
- Join us in weekly chats with authors, readers and other guests
- Get writing guidelines
- AND MUCH MORE!

Visit our website at
http://www.kensingtonbooks.com

THE
ELIGIBLE
MISS
ELLIOTT

Victoria Hinshaw

ZEBRA BOOKS
Kensington Publishing Corp.
http://kensingtonbooks.com

One

Miss Rosalind Elliott nuzzled the silky ear of the King Charles spaniel in her lap and stroked his back, willing the squirming dog to calm down. She perched beside her grandmother, Anne, Lady Rotherford, on a peach satin sofa in the drawing room of a graceful stone house on Gay Street. Lady Rotherford held another wiggling dog, nearly identical in coloring. If they had much of a wait before they met Bath's premier portraitist, both Pip and Popsy would writhe away their meticulous grooming.

Lady Rotherford looked around the room with an appraising air, as if assigning a monetary value to the furnishings. Rosalind followed her gaze from the gilt sconces beside the windows to the thick jewel tones of the Axminster carpet to the carved marble fruit on the fireplace surround. Beyond the double doors at the rear of the salon, Rosalind could see a library with an entrance to a rear garden.

Lady Rotherford pronounced herself satisfied. "Mr. Haeffer has a most elegant place here. He has certainly come up in the world since he painted us."

"That was a long time ago, Grandmama," Rosalind said, brushing her cheek over Pip's head.

"Of course. Why, you were only a babe in your mother's arms. To think how well he has done in twenty-five years! Now, sit still, Popsy, my pet, you little rascal. Jason Haeffer is the only artist who can capture the quality of your adorable little face, so you better be on your best behavior."

Rosalind smiled at the way both dogs watched their mistress with huge liquid brown eyes, snuffling and quivering in anticipation of a treat.

Through the half open door to the foyer, she heard footsteps coming downstairs and the voice of Mr. Clarence, assistant to the artist.

"Captain Chadwell, if you will wait in the library, we will bring Lady Charlotte down when she has changed."

"What?" Lady Rotherford gasped, her mouth gaping wide in a face flushed red with irritation. "Not that wretched rake Chadwell in Bath! Good heavens, what could he be doing here? I am shocked that libertine would have the audacity to show his face here in Bath. I suppose he is with Isiline. She is such an old snake she is sure to upset everything!"

"Grandmama, do not overset yourself. You need have nothing to do with either the captain or Lady Isiline."

The dogs continued to wiggle and beg, but to Rosalind's amazement, her grandmother fumed on, too agitated to attend to her pets. Clearly Lady Rotherford's sad rift with her old friend stung painfully. Their families had been friends for decades. The Captain Chadwell Grandmama was so horrified about had been a childhood playmate of Rosalind's.

"How dare they come to Bath?" Lady Rotherford clutched Rosalind's arm. "You have not seen Lady

Isiline Aldercote since you were just a child, but she has become an utter antidote. Back then, Philip was merely a very naughty lad, though already a disgrace to his family. Not that any of those Aldercotes live up to their breeding."

"Grandmother, everyone comes to Bath." Perhaps it was time to heal the schism once and for all, Rosalind thought. Bringing them together again, curing their disgust of one another, would not be easy. From the depth of her grandmother's distress, Rosalind could see how much Lady Rotherford missed her lifelong friend. "You were the best of friends with Lady Isiline, were you not?"

"Those were the days before I knew her true character. As for her nephew, being away in uncivilized parts of the globe in the navy must have well fit his character. Despicable ruffian."

"Shhh. He is just in the next room. I am surprised to hear you speak so of one of the King's own officers."

"Humph!" Lady Rotherford in her distraction let go of Popsy, who plopped to the floor and scampered off.

Pip lunged out of Rosalind's arms and raced away after his mate.

"Oh, catch them, Rosalind! Hurry." Lady Rotherford waved her lace-mittened hands in the air. "They are such fragile creatures."

Rosalind dropped her reticule and dashed after the dogs. *Fragile, nonsense. They are about as fragile as a pair of draft horses.*

At the end of the salon, the dogs tore through the barely ajar double doors and into the library, heading directly for the entrance to the garden. Rosalind shoved one door aside and ran after them. The little beasts were so spoiled they never behaved, and she always was the one who had to give chase.

"Whoa there, pup." A man's voice, a deep and husky voice, sounded from outside.

The spaniels sped through the door and down the steps. The man in the garden reached down and scooped up one unruly dog.

"Oh, thank you," Rosalind said. "So very kind . . ."

He thrust the spaniel into her arms and started after the other dog, which had bolted past him in a flash and scampered onto the garden's gravel path.

She had only a brief view of his face, but she would have known him anywhere. This was how Philip Chadwell had grown up, tall, wide shouldered, with a voice like a smooth cello. And a face that was not quite handsome but forcefully compelling in a way that easily met the physical requirements for the appellation of rakehell.

Rosalind handed Popsy into Mr. Clarence's arms and hastened down the steps. Pip, his head cocked to one side and his tail wagging furiously, stood a few feet from Chadwell, waiting for him to give chase. Pip barked twice, obviously delighted to be out-of-doors, and darted away as soon as the captain took a step.

Rosalind took the other side of the garden and approached the spaniel around a manicured border surrounding a tall urn. She was one step away from seizing him when Pip whirled around and flashed by her, going the opposite direction.

"You slyboots!" Rosalind halted, confused about whether to keep running after him or coax him into her clutches. The dog stopped precisely halfway around the circular border from her, wagged his plumed tail, and barked again. His favorite game . . . but she had no ball for Pip to chase. She took a deep breath and pushed her bonnet back and off her head. Elbows wide and fists at her waist, she stared at the silly beast. "Come here, Pip, this very moment."

Her stern voice only caused the dog to jump and paw the air with his short front legs, then bark even harder. He was ready to play.

"It's a full-fledged mutiny, I'd say. But if you go one way and I go the other, we'll capture the scoundrel."

Captain Chadwell's deep voice carried a whiff of humor, and she looked at him with more than a touch of irritation. He was laughing at her again, exactly as he had done years and years ago. Just as he had done when he chased her with a toad across the park at Rotherford House when she was about eight years old.

For a moment they stared across the hedges at each other. With a twinge of amusement, she saw a look of recognition dawn on his face, on his very tanned and ruggedly attractive face. His eyes were deep gray with flecks of green that must glow when he was on the sunlit sea. His dark hair was ruffled, his clothing undistinguished, yet he had an unmistakable aura of strength and authority.

Pip barked even louder, then charged past her, cutting the garden circle into thirds.

"Come, Pip," Rosalind cooed, edging toward the dog. "Here, boy, come to me."

Silently, Captain Chadwell stalked Pip from his direction.

Just as she was about to make the capture, Pip dived into the bushes, emerging beside a clump of

daisies which he promptly flattened, hopping up
and down with a look of pure joy in his bulging
dark eyes.

Rosalind stopped beside Captain Chadwell, flustered and quite disheveled. She felt inappropriately
warm and appropriately wary, uncomfortably conscious of both her disarray and her closeness to him.

"Does he fetch?" Chadwell asked.

"Why yes, but I have no ball to throw."

"Try this." He took out a large white handkerchief,
knotted it, and tucking the ends into the knot, gave
it to Rosalind.

"Here, Pip. Fetch!" She waved the makeshift ball
at the dog then tossed it toward the house.

Pip raced toward it and pounced. Captain Chadwell snatched him up and tried to dislodge the
once-pristine linen from between Pip's jaws. Without
success.

Rosalind winced as she heard the fabric tear.
"Oh, I am so sorry, Captain."

"A mere scrap, sacrificed to the cause." He
handed her the dog and bowed. "A pleasure to see
you again, Rosalind."

Her cheeks warmed, and she silently cursed her
missish tendency to blush. She very much wished
she looked her best, cool and serene in a silken
gown instead of hot and rumpled in a wrinkled
muslin. "I thank you for your gallant rescue, Captain Chadwell."

"Oh, Rosalind, Rosalind, bring Pip to Mama,"
Lady Rotherford called from the steps.

"I must go . . ." Rosalind dipped a little curtsy and
hurried back to the house. Glancing back more than
once, she saw the captain sit on an iron bench, lean

back, and stretch out his legs. Just inside the library, she handed the panting dog to her grandmother.

"Pip, you naughty, naughty boy! You've lost your ribbons and you are full of twigs and leaves." Lady Rotherford marched back into the drawing room, keeping up a steady discourse all the way. "Pip, I don't know which is worse, your getting all messy or poor Rosalind having to talk with that despicable Chadwell fellow."

Rosalind followed, about to object, but Mr. Clarence met them in the center of the room. "Mr. Haeffer is ready to see you, milady."

"I'll wait down here, Grandmother," Rosalind said. "I need to fasten up my hair."

"Be sure to stay away from that unscrupulous reprobate out there."

"Oh, I am certain he is leaving."

"Take care to avoid him," Lady Rotherford said. "You have your reputation to think of." She started up the stairs in the company of Mr. Clarence.

Still heated from her exertions, Rosalind removed her pelisse and shook out the skirt of her simple sprigged muslin gown. She took a little brush from her reticule and went to one of the tall mirrors above a gilded pier table. Where should she start, she wondered, contemplating the disordered strands of honey gold hair that floated around her face.

She was not sure how long he had been in the room when she finally noticed Captain Chadwell inside the double doors. He lounged against the wall, both hands behind his back, as if studying her.

"My thanks for your assistance, Captain." She felt her cheeks glowing, but refused to become rattled again.

"My pleasure," he replied. "Do you need any help pinning up the back?"

A little gasp escaped her. "No, thank you. My bonnet will cover . . ." She felt behind her back. "Now what happened to my bonnet?"

He swung it out from behind him. "I rescued it from the lilac branches." He came closer, but did not offer her the hat. "I fear you are no more careful of your apparel than you were as a child."

She grinned. "As I recall, you chased me into that mud in fear of my life. That was my best white dress I ruined."

He walked over to the sofa and placed the bonnet beside her pelisse. "I like you much better without the chapeau anyway."

Instinctively she touched her hair again.

He sauntered over to the mirror and stood beside her. "Your grandmother warned you not to speak to me."

"Grandmother spoke quite out of turn. I think she was flustered to see you in Bath." Flustered was exactly the way Rosalind felt as she twisted a curl around her finger.

"I am surprised to be here myself. I am attending my great-aunt, Lady Isiline. We arrived last week."

"Why Bath?" She watched him looking at her in the mirror as she ineffectually fiddled with her windblown hair.

"I have several missions to accomplish here. One is to have my sister Lady Charlotte's portrait done. Another is to enroll her in school. Actually, Charlotte is my half sister, a mere eight years old. My third mission is to escort my aunt to the Pump Room and see to her comfort."

"But we have not seen you there." Rosalind felt

the power of his gaze as though she were a tiny skiff sailing into the eye of a frigate's cannon.

"We go after the morning rush. My aunt tells me Bath is full of parvenus and cits."

"She has not been in Bath for several years."

"True." His grin was slightly crooked and rather captivating.

"Do you know why she has not been coming?"

"I have been away for many years. I have no idea." He reached over and pulled a pin from her hair. "Take them all out. It looks lovely down."

Rosalind stopped herself from drawing away in alarm. She had no idea how to respond to his familiarity.

"Can I help you?" He was so close she could feel his breath on her neck as he pulled out another hairpin.

She quickly grabbed the rest of them and let her hair fall free. Her heartbeat resounded in her ears and her hands coiled so tightly the pins almost cut into her palms.

He handed her the two pins he had removed and took a step back, propping one arm on the pier table.

Rosalind forced herself back to the conversation. "I suspect your great-aunt has not come to Bath lately because my grandmother spends most of the year here. Lady Rotherford and Lady Isiline have been feuding for the last three or four years."

"Whatever should those two have to squabble about?"

"I don't know. But my grandmother never goes to London anymore, nor does she visit friends near Lady Isiline's home in Berkshire."

Chadwell stroked his chin. "Aunt Izzy never

mentioned a problem, though I have noticed she is reluctant to go about freely in Bath. She came here only because Dr. Loomis was highly recommended. The fellow is probably a quack, but she thinks he is capable of effecting miracle cures. What caused the rift?"

"Grandmother refuses to discuss the matter. Captain Chadwell, I wish the ladies could end their feud. They went to school together and were friends for decades. It is most sad they no longer speak."

He shrugged. "Is it not the custom of elderly persons to conceive elaborate disputes from time to time?"

She took a step closer to him. "You may be unmoved by my grandmother's distress, but you must be responsive to Lady Isiline's lamentable exclusion from those circles she once relished."

"I expect she will find new acquaintances."

The man was as exasperating as he was attractive. Rosalind sat down on the sofa. "I will be disappointed, Captain Chadwell, if you will not assist me in ending the feud."

He took the gilt chair next to her. "Why should I want to do that? If I were to assist you, Miss Elliott . . ." He smiled and winked. "I can think of many tasks both of us might find more deserving of our efforts."

Rosalind bristled at his innuendo. Not only was he trying to provoke her, apparently the captain had no interest in making his aunt's life more agreeable. He was every bit the rascal he had been as a child. Perhaps she would have more success by appealing to his self-interest. She leaned toward him.

"I should think if you are the sole companion of your great-aunt, you should hardly have a moment to call your own. However, if she enjoys spending time with other ladies, conversing, attending card parties and the like, her amusement will no longer fall exclusively upon your shoulders. You might be relieved of the entire weight of her attention."

He smiled and raised his eyebrows. She wondered if he was on the verge of laughter or whether a storm was brewing over her interference. She forged ahead.

"If the feud continues, the predicament might come to dominate all her time and thus yours. Seeking an ally here, a supporter there, taking sides on every spiteful tiff that occurs to the questionably worthy denizens of the Pump Room. All carried out with malicious spirit instead of harmless curiosity. Your life will become a most disagreeable muddle."

"I begin to get your point."

"If I were you, I would be most anxious to reintroduce Lady Isiline to the delights of what Bath is all about—the genteel gatherings of the comfortably well off to concentrate upon the discussion of their ailments, both real and imaginary, in an atmosphere of cordiality. Certainly the ending of the feud would accommodate this."

"Bravo, Miss Elliott. I surrender to your infinitely superior perception."

She shoved her long curls back over her shoulder. "Then you will help?"

"I see I have no alternative if I am to have a moment's peace. So I have another mission. Or rather we have a joint mission. We must clear up the misunderstanding and reunite our respective relations." His smile had a rather wicked glint.

She wished she were not so fascinated by his eyes.

"Thank you. Our first task is to find the cause of the disagreement. That might facilitate a cure."

"I wager Aunt Izzy's abigail knows the story, but I hesitate to involve servants."

"I agree. Perhaps I can address the subject directly with my grandmother. We must take care to keep our goal secret and our efforts concealed, do you not agree?"

"Secret? Why?"

"I know my grandmother. She is, to be honest, quite stubborn. I suspect Lady Isiline is equally intractable. If either of them suspects we are trying to bring them together, our task will be doubly difficult. And in a place like Bath, if we are seen so much as speaking to each other, that fact is likely to reach the ears of one or both of the ladies almost instantly. Leading to all sorts of questions and suspicions on their part. If that happens, I suspect we will never get the situation remedied."

"Yes, I see. So this will be a secret mission?"

"Unless you find that too comical . . ."

"On the contrary. I yield to your command. You set the course and I shall follow in your wake." Captain Chadwell smiled and bowed, as if to seal their bargain.

Rosalind curtsied in return, then lifted her gaze to his. The green flecks in his gray eyes glowed in the bright light, emphasizing the mischievous look he wore.

He reached for her hand and drew it to his lips. Her breath caught in her throat. Sharp tingles ran up and down her arm. She had never before felt such a sudden rush of exhilaration.

When he released her hand, she drew it to her cheek, then felt her blush deepen. Like a silly ninny.

His smile seemed all too casual for the intensity of her reaction. "I would like to see the garden again," he said. "Lady Charlotte takes more time at her toilette than most women ten times her years. Do you have time for a turn around the path?"

"Of course I do." What possessed her? She ought to be running away from these strange feelings. She ought to be putting her hair back in its topknot. She ought to be seeing if she could help her grandmother. Instead she was following Captain Philip Chadwell through the library and into the brightness of early afternoon.

"Have you ever had your portrait painted, Rosalind? Or, Miss Elliott, I should more properly call you."

Thankfully he had a normal subject at hand. Her mind was a blank. "I was painted by Mr. Haeffer, as a matter of fact, with my mother and grandmother. I was an infant at the time."

"Ah," he said. "As was I, in a white dress and long dark curls."

Rosalind smiled and almost spoke aloud. How beautiful he must have been. "Hardly the scamp you became later?"

"On the contrary, even in infancy, they say my dresses were always dirty and grass-stained, my face and hands filthy, and my hair full of snarls and sticky with jam."

"Oh, not really."

"I was the naughtiest of the brothers, and my nurse called me a demon."

She wondered if that name had stuck. She had only the vaguest memories of what she'd heard about him, of some scandal when he was home from the sea.

He folded her hand into his elbow as they walked. "That is why they sent me into the navy at age twelve. But I assure you, Miss Elliott, I am considerably reformed and now have left His Majesty's Service no more to prowl the coasts of France."

"But why?"

"Peace is indeed unkind to my ilk, for it leaves us with no better duties than assisting elderly ladies to take the waters and helping little girls find suitable schooling."

"But, sir, are you serious? Do you mean you have left the sea for good?"

"As long as I am in land-locked Bath, the oceans are only siren songs in my head. I think I may someday find a fine little yawl to sail on Tor Bay. As for the Royal Navy, they wanted to put me into an office at the Admiralty. I declined."

"Captain Chadwell," Mr. Clarence called from the house. "Please come quickly. Lady Charlotte is feeling poorly."

"I shall be right there." The captain turned to Rosalind. "We shall meet tomorrow? Is Barratt's Library suitable?"

"About ten? Bond Street is not too busy at an early hour."

"Ten it shall be. I look forward to our literary rendezvous."

The thought left her heart dancing.

"Mr. Haeffer was exceedingly cordial. He agreed with very little effort on my part to paint Pip and Popsy." Lady Rotherford sat before a tea tray in her Rose Salon, as she had christened her drawing room done up entirely in shades of pink, ivory, and gold.

"I am so pleased to hear it," Rosalind said.

Lady Rotherford tossed a few crumbs of her cake to Pip and Popsy, who watched her every move from their satin cushion. "I have learned that indeed Lady Isiline is back in Bath, as vituperative as ever, with that odious Chadwell fellow and an appalling female child who screeched when she saw my dear ones posing in the studio. Such a ruckus! You would have thought she were being attacked. More evidence of bad breeding in that family, I declare."

Rosalind suppressed a smile. "So Lady Isiline will be about the town, I suppose."

"Can you imagine anything more calamitous? Our summer will be ruined. She will try to gain the ear of my friends and she will slander me with lie after scandalous lie. You can count on it." Lady Rotherford stirred more sugar into her tea.

"But perhaps—"

"No doubt Chadwell will find a rich widow. His misbehavior with the Countess of DeMuth was abominable."

"When was that?" Rosalind had only the faintest recollection of hearing the name. She dared not ask more, however much she secretly wished to hear the whole story.

"Oh, I do not remember. He will not have improved after years of putting into exotic ports where foreign women are . . . not a proper subject for either of us."

"We could not possibly know . . ."

"His father married a gel almost young enough to be his granddaughter. I tell you, Rosalind, bad breeding runs in families!"

Rosalind almost choked keeping a straight face.

Lady Rotherford set down her cup and rose, all the while continuing to talk without a break. "I would not lower myself to resort to Isiline's tactics, indeed I would not. Spreading rumors and making the most sinister judgments out of mere tarradiddle. I cannot allow that old shrew to spread falsehoods."

Lady Rotherford, a glint in her eye, paced the length of her drawing room. "We shall have to make several calls this very afternoon. I believe we should start with Georgiana and Sophia. If there is anyone as important to the first circles in Bath as I am, they are the ones. We must work quickly to prevent the damage Isiline will try to do. I shall go upstairs immediately and prepare a list of those I must see."

Lady Rotherford marched out of the room with the importance of Her Goal revealed in every stride. Pip and Popsy scrambled after her.

Rosalind wished she could think of some way to deter her grandmother's quest. Things could only worsen if she stirred up old gossip. Yet if Rosalind went along and listened intently, she might learn the original cause of the rift. Then she would have something to report to Captain Chadwell in the morning.

Perhaps he would have some luck in that regard himself. Captain Chadwell . . . she recalled his shockingly attractive countenance and his tall, well-formed build. They had known one another as children, though other than the toad-chasing incident, she had few clear memories. Had their parents been friends, or just her grandmother and Lady Isiline?

As the youngest brother, he probably turned into a demon in pure self-defense. Years of service in the navy should have gone far to wipe his slate clean, except for whatever he had done to earn his standing as a rake. Of course, none of her grandmother's friends was likely to report favorable accounts of his achievements. The story of the Countess of DeMuth would be appropriately recollected and embellished. Rosalind closed her eyes and tried to still the advance in her heartbeat. Why ever did it matter? She was acting like a green girl indeed.

"The post, Miss Elliott." Lady Rotherford's butler presented her with two letters.

"Thank you, Jaspers." If ever there was a welcome distraction . . . She took the letters and curled up in the corner of a sofa. The first one was from her man of business, and she scanned it quickly, noticing only that the investment news was positive. The second letter was from her best friend, Delphine. She unfolded it, surprised to see the page crossed and recrossed with rapid handwriting, quite unlike Delphine's usual careful script.

As she read, her heart grew heavy and her mood darkened though the words she read brought news of joy. Delphine was in love and, after only a short acquaintance, about to be married to a wonderful man. She required Rosalind to wish her happy and invited her to attend the wedding.

Rosalind let the letter slide to the floor as her shoulders slumped and she groped for a hanky. What a dreadfully selfish reaction, she thought. I should be thrilled for her, delighted she has found a fine match, not crying over my isolation and loneliness.

She bit down on her lip and straightened her back. She and Delphine once had plans. After their last shared Season, in which neither of them had a single prospective suitor she cared for, Rosalind and Delphine pledged to set up an establishment together someday, when Rosalind no longer had Grandmother to tend and Delphine's sisters were suitably launched. After all, Rosalind had reasoned, of what good was her money if she could not use it for her own happiness?

What had made her particularly eager was relief from the cloying attention of one fortune hunter after another. There never seemed to be any eligible partners who were not thoroughly engrossed in discovering the extent of her wealth.

Twice in the last four years she had considered offers from gentlemen. Neither had engaged her affection or her intellect, and she found a future living in comfort with Delphine to be far more appealing.

Now Delphine would not figure into her life. She reached down and retrieved the letters from the rug, peering again at the message from her man of business. More canal building and now something to do with bridges. There was little comfort in being found worthy by one's man of business to hear the details of commerce. Transportation, he once told her, would bring England prosperity. At the moment, one had to wonder . . .

As for being rich, wealth hardly seemed an advantage for a female. She rested her head on the carved sofa back and gritted her teeth. *Oh, Delphine,* she thought, *I am truly happy for you. I cannot begrudge your discovery of love. Love is what I wanted once. Now, down deep, I still do, even after my discouraging experiences.*

Rosalind sighed and refolded her letters. Could

a wealthy woman ever trust any gentleman who pursued her?

What was that ridiculous aphorism of her grandmother's, the one that fractured the vicar's favorite biblical passage? "Can a rich man pass through the eye of a needle?" For her, it was, "Could a rich woman find true love?"

She tried to shrug off the dilemma and return to the immediate agenda. Dear Grandmother and her mystifying jumble of ideas. Some such misunderstanding must be the root of the estrangement between her and Lady Isiline. Somehow, Rosalind mused, she and Captain Chadwell would find the source of the breach and sort out the ladies' aversion to one another. When she made calls with Grandmother later, she would listen for hints of the quarrel's origins.

To Delphine, Rosalind would write the warmest of congratulations.

Two

"Lottie, my dear, please don't cry," Captain Chadwell said for the twentieth time since they had left Mr. Haeffer's house. "Dry your eyes before you see Auntie or she will become distraught." *And blame me for not protecting the silly chit*, he thought.

Lady Charlotte gave a big sigh and shuddered. Her eyes were red and puffy, her lower lip quivering with sobs. Her little handkerchief was practically shredded, his having earlier met its fate.

As they approached the door of Lady Isiline's boudoir, Captain Chadwell tried to straighten Lottie's hair ribbons, but she shrugged him away. Nothing, he supposed, would do except a full-fledged tantrum. He wished he could simply open the door for the child, close it behind her, escape to his own quarters, and be alone.

Instead, he followed her as Charlotte erupted into Lady Isiline's presence with wails of fright.

"Auntie," she cried, "there were vicious dogs and they tried to bite me." She collapsed into Lady Isiline's arms, whimpering sorrowfully.

Captain Chadwell met Lady Isiline's questioning look. "After Lady Charlotte had her sitting, she changed in another room. When she emerged, Haeffer was trying to pose two little spaniels. She became quite upset, though I don't think either of them did more than bark a little at her from across the room."

"Why didn't you shield her, Philip?" Lady Isiline asked. "After all, you know the child is terrified of animals. There, there, dear. Nothing will hurt you here."

Captain Chadwell controlled the urge to express his opinion of how his father and his father's henwit of a wife had allowed their daughter to become so peculiar. He strongly suspected Lottie's malady was nothing but a technique to gain attention from her parents. Or in this case, from her overly indulgent aunt.

"Call for a footman to bring us some tea and sweets, Philip," Lady Isiline ordered.

"Honey cakes and currant buns and white custard," Lottie managed to demand through her tears.

A few minutes later, once the child was plied with sweetmeats, Philip could see she recovered. He gratefully took his unexpected brandy, and handed a glass of sherry to Lady Isiline. "You are a master of improvisation, Gar," he said to the footman. "Thank you."

Lady Isiline sipped her sherry, then turned to Philip with a questioning look. "Now I must know what kind of dogs were in Mr. Haeffer's studio."

Lottie, her mouth half full of pink cake, responded without hesitation. "They had big bulgy eyes and snarly teeth and—"

"A pair of King Charles Spaniels which Mr. Haeffer is painting."

A look of rage grew on Lady Isiline's face. "I know of only one woman in Bath who would have the audacity to require the services of Mr. Haeffer to paint her wretched beasts."

Philip refused to rise to her bait. He strolled over to the window and stared down at the garden. The blooming lilacs reminded him of how Miss Elliott's bonnet had slipped down her back and got caught on a branch she coaxed the dog to behave. The sun had turned her tawny hair to spun gold. Her movements were accomplished with surprising grace and offered multiple glimpses of the lady's shapely ankles.

Lady Isiline's forbidding tone knocked him back to the present.

"Did you see that malicious harpy?" she asked.

"If you are referring to Lady Rotherford, I did."

"More to the point, did she see you?"

"Yes, I believe she did."

"Oh, I never should have come to Bath. Her viper's tongue will spread her bitterness against me in every drawing room in town."

"What is a malicious harpy?" Lottie asked, looking up from her cake.

Philip stifled a laugh. "When you study your Greek, you will learn about harpies."

"Mama says I will never need to learn Greek."

"Quite so," he said. "Perhaps you will not need to learn it. But perhaps you will develop an interest in the classics." *And perhaps you will climb the Matterhorn.*

Lottie threw him a doubtful look before she bit into another biscuit.

Philip turned his attention to Lady Isiline, who held out her glass for more sherry. He carried the decanter to her and spoke in a whisper. "Later please explain your hostility toward Lady Rotherford. I do not understand why you hold her in such strong aversion."

His aunt took a large swallow from her refilled glass. "The story fills me with revulsion. I do not wish to repeat it."

"If it is to affect our sojourn here, I am in need of edification. Now I shall leave you ladies until later this afternoon when we go to Dr. Loomis." He bowed to each of them and left the room. As he closed the door, he heard Lottie's voice.

"He never did tell me about the malicious harpy . . ."

"Fanny, how good of you to receive me." Rosalind entered the book-lined room that served as Fanny's study.

As F. T. Gilmore, Fanny published popular books on the history of the four hundred years of Roman rule in Britain. Though she was at least a decade older than Rosalind, the two had become good friends. Rosalind admired Fanny, and particularly enjoyed their occasional forays to inspect nearby discoveries of Roman or Celtic objects so often found when men dug into the earth of Somersetshire.

Clad in her usual sober brown round gown, Fanny gave Rosalind a welcoming hug. "I am delighted to have you visit any time. Please sit down and take off your bonnet."

Rosalind noted the heavy volume Fanny set on the drum table beside her. "I do not mean to interrupt your research. I was out walking and found myself wanting to ask you a question."

"I am glad for the break. I am nodding off over this very dry and very dull tome by a fellow who had no pity for his readers. I despise writers who try harder to overwhelm their audience with their Latin vocabulary than with the quality of their findings."

"You are reading in Latin?"

"Ha! That would be much easier than the so-called English this fellow pretended to use. It is a history of the Romans in Britain done in Cromwell's time. One can only take joy from the thought that this author might have lost his head after the Restoration. Charles the Second might well have condemned him for mind-numbing prose. Unfortunately I doubt the merry monarch was quite blood-thirsty enough to attack the scholars, however dreadful their work."

Rosalind laughed. "Only you, Fanny, would imagine such a thing."

"Perhaps. But when I am wading through the text, it pleases me to visualize various tortures for this fellow. Hanging would surely not have been enough. But what is it you want to ask me, Ros?"

"You have been in Bath for more than five years, have you not?"

Fanny nodded and pushed a footstool over to Rosalind. "I arrived in 1810, as a matter of fact."

"Thank you." Rosalind propped up her feet and removed her bonnet. "I know your abhorrence of gossip, but I wonder if you remember a little flurry over the quarrel between my grandmother and Lady Isiline Aldercote? It must have been quite the cause célèbre at the time, for they had been good friends forever."

"I am afraid I am the wrong person to ask. I pay little attention to the scandal-mongering in the Pump Room. That is, if I can escape the usual *on-dit* of the morning."

"I am looking for a dispassionate onlooker who might remember the original spat."

"I suppose you do not dare ask the aggrieved parties."

"Grandmother will not speak of it. But I am sure she secretly wishes to repair the damage."

A plump tiger cat strolled into the room, waving high its black-tipped tail.

Fanny reached out to stroke the animal. "Here is my wonderful Juno. Apparently she got out and found her Jupiter some time ago, for she presented me with three kittens last month."

Rosalind paid her homage to Juno as the cat rubbed against her leg. "I love cats. I had several at Fosswell, and I miss them."

"Perhaps you would like one of mine, or all three. They are adorable and I suspect Juno is ready to rid herself of them. I have to close them up in my bed-chamber or they would be all over the house."

"I wish I could take one, but Grandmother's dogs are quite the rulers in our abode. I doubt they would take well to the presence of a usurper."

"But at least you must see them. Perhaps you will be unable to resist."

Fanny led the way upstairs to her room and cautiously opened the door. Three furry balls spilled into the hall.

"They hear me coming and lean on the door, the little rogues."

Rosalind picked up the gray kitten nosing at her half boots. For some reason the smoky color and bright green eyes reminded her of Philip Chadwell. Why such a ridiculous thought came into her head, she could not imagine. She dragged her thoughts back to the kitten. "How precious. Look, she has all four white feet."

"I suspect that one is a 'he' and it seems he will grow to be quite the Caesar. Look at the size of those paws."

Rosalind snuggled him to her chin. "Juno's Jupiter must have been a real tiger."

"I must admit I get a chuckle out of thinking of her selecting the strongest and proudest as her mate. But, typical male he must be, for you do not see him hanging around helping out with the babies."

Rosalind did not want to get into a discussion about men. Fanny held the entire gender in low esteem, an opinion Rosalind did not share, at least not completely. She set little Caesar down. "If I were you, I would not part with any of them."

Fanny produced a length of string that the kittens tumbled over each other to bat. "Who would believe it? F. T. Gilmore, the spinster scholar herself, playing with kittens and string?"

Rosalind and Fanny sat on the carpet and watched the little cats bounce and wriggle over one another, pouncing on the string and nibbling at its tip. After half an hour, Juno stepped into their midst and took up one kitten by the scruff of its neck.

"Mama thinks they have had enough." Fanny picked up another kitten and followed Juno to their basket.

Rosalind brought Caesar and set him beside the others. "Why, Fanny, you have put them on your cashmere shawl."

"I have indeed. I wanted them to have the softest bed, but I never thought it would be ruined, full of snags from their little claws."

They shut the door on Juno as she stretched out to let her babies nurse.

"I have kept you from your work long enough." Rosalind gathered up her bonnet and gloves. "Grandmother will be wondering where I have gone."

Fanny accompanied her to the door. "I will try to remember if I heard anything about your two ladies, Ros, but I do not hold out much hope. Even when I was a novice in Bath, I disregarded most of the palaver that passes for conversation in the Pump Room. If you change your mind about those kittens . . ."

"Thank you, Fanny. Even though my curiosity is still unsatisfied, I enjoyed the afternoon."

Captain Chadwell finished the last of his dinner wine and set the goblet on the table. How had he come to this? Three days confined in Bath, obliged by his very own pledge to involve himself in the exact circumstances he despised most, a bumblebroth of meaningless gossip and ancient grudges. A month becalmed in the relentless sun of the tropics could not have scorched his brain more efficiently.

Could he find a way to approach his great-aunt about the source of her feud? Nary a single initiative came to mind. He needed a strategy, a way of approaching the subject indirectly to persuade Lady Isiline to discuss the past, something she had resolutely sworn to evade. Over dinner he had broached the subject of her old friend Lady Rotherford, only to receive a furious tongue-lashing for his impudence.

Instead of approaching the enemy fleet head on,

perhaps he needed to take an oblique tack and come at the topic from a different perspective. Make it a family matter?

He sighed and pushed his chair back from the table. Why was a naval man such as himself, who had attacked the King's enemies, commandeered their ships and imprisoned their crews, why now was he in danger of sinking because of a ludicrous squabble between elderly ladies? Or more accurately, because of a rash promise to a certain young lady.

Philip joined his great-aunt in the drawing room, where she sat before her embroidery frame, yet set no stitches; instead she stared away into the darkness beyond the window.

"Has Charlotte gone up?"

Lady Isiline turned her pale blue eyes on him. "Some time ago. I thought perhaps you had gone from the table to the library. What were you doing so long?"

"Thinking. Thinking about you and your old friends. What happened between our family and the Elliotts?"

"Between the families? Nothing. But as far as that old gabble-monger Lady Rotherford is concerned, she spreads vicious rumors, however incorrect."

"About what?" He sat on the striped satin sofa and stretched out his legs.

"About anybody who does not agree with her warped views."

"And that includes you?"

"Philip, I told you I shall not discuss the woman or her friends. There is no reason to bring up old lies and air them all over again."

"You were best friends."

Lady Isiline glowered at him. "How she managed

to hide her true nature from me for so long is a matter of great distress to me. I thought I was a better judge of character than to have been her bosom bow for so many years. I never saw her true and treacherous nature."

"How did you discover her, ah, deceit?"

"That would be deceits, multiple wicked deceits! She is downright malicious." Lady Isiline abruptly rediscovered her needle and jabbed it into her embroidery with a growl of anger. "How am I to accomplish this flower if you keep chattering like those vindictive biddies in the Pump Room?"

Philip suppressed a chuckle. This approach was yielding only a litany of supposed traits, hardly a basis for the conflict. "So what dreadful things did she make up about you?"

"Ha! Nothing that came close to the truth. Nothing but lies that do not bear repeating." Her face was set in a fierce scowl.

"But surely you told people she was in error—"

"Philip! Now, if you would just move that candle stand a bit closer to me, you may leave me in peace."

He followed her instruction, and stood looking over her shoulder. "But surely you must wish to—"

"I wish to keep these silks untangled! And to cease this blather about matters long ago over and done."

"Then I beg your pardon for raising the subject. I only hoped you would rediscover some of your old friends whose company might bring you pleasure. I hoped to relieve you from my lack of social acceptance and from the occasional frets of Lady Charlotte."

Lady Isiline's face softened. "You need not worry about me, Philip. Though I appreciate your kindness, I do not need your sympathy or your attempts to reverse ancient history. I am here only for Charlotte's sake and to see Dr. Loomis, not to reestablish myself in the good graces of the passel of old hens and worn-down valetudinarians that passes for Bath society."

"Aunt Isiline, you are a lady of commanding presence and I bow to your wishes." *You are also as stubborn as a cantankerous old mule,* he added silently. "I shall take a brief stroll before I go up. Sleep well."

"Take care not to catch a chill. Good night, Philip."

Once outside, Philip drew the fresh night air deep into his lungs. He was not a man cut out for overheated drawing rooms and the crochets of elderly ladies. He felt at home out of doors, with the stars winking overhead and the moon masked by a haze of thin clouds. He wanted nothing more than to get away from Bath and establish his own modest property, a place he could call his own, from which he could easily reach the sea. He had taken great pains to conceal the extent of the fortune he had earned from prizes taken during his naval service. He invested quietly, and few of his acquaintances were aware of his good luck. Once he had finished with his obligations to his father regarding Charlotte's schooling, he would be free to search out and purchase a suitable estate near the coast.

He was finished with fighting at sea or any place else. Never again would he fire a pistol or swing his sword at another human being. He had seen enough blood and horror to last several lifetimes. Nor could he tolerate a post in the Admiralty, cooped up in London writing dispatches.

He had no complaints. He was a very fortunate man to have escaped the war with no serious wounds. Many of his old friends had not been so lucky. Now all he wanted was a quiet life in the country, and he had earned the blunt to support a modest property. He planned to buy a small yacht, to moor it near his home. He could have the best of both land and sea, free to choose whichever suited him on any given day.

He would not miss the command of the men. Leadership had its rewards but also its difficulties. Discipline had to be strict aboard a naval vessel, yet he had despised the cruelty of the lashings. He had never reconciled himself to losing his men in battle or to reading the Scriptures as the bodies were sewn into canvas and sent to the depths.

The freshening wind in his hair, the spray of saltwater on his face, the lurch forward as sails unfurled and the gusts caught hold, the feeling of freedom and speed, these were the gifts of the sea to the seaman. These were the gifts he had the means to enjoy now, to repeat whenever he wished. He was a fortunate man indeed.

He welcomed the solitude he would soon have. Eventually he might long for the camaraderie he had shared with a few of the other officers. If he were entirely honest with himself, he would have to admit his occasional yearning for the company of a woman, not only to slake his physical lusts, but to share a different kind of companionship than what he'd experienced with his men. This kind of closeness he had rarely seen, but when in its presence, he had keenly wished for it.

One of his fellow captains on the North Sea watch had such a relationship with his wife. Seeing them together engendered his wish to know their kind of love, with desire much deeper than passion, the desire that marked the completion of a circle or that matched one half of a pair with its twin. Bentley had called it fulfillment, though Philip could not put a precise name to the notion.

He turned the corner onto Broad Street, still busy with carriages and drays. Why bother to ruminate in such a direction? He had long ago destroyed his right to the privilege of approaching a respectable woman. How cavalierly he had thrown away his good name by running away with Lady DeMuth.

The affair had lasted but four days before she found another man, a Frenchman with courtly charms and a fat purse. She and Philip had barely reached Paris before she dumped him at their modest inn to run away again with some silk-clad courtier and move into a palatial town house where her husband eventually caught up with her.

But Philip's was the name that was whispered all over London and among the hundreds of English holiday makers in Paris during the brief Peace of Amiens more than a dozen years ago. Somehow, the story went, that French *comte*, or whoever he was, became the rescuer of the lady. However erroneous the legend, not he, not the lady, not her husband nor the Frenchman ever set the story straight. Lady DeMuth had used him, mere boy that he was, to get to Paris, where her husband had refused to take her. Then, in an amazing sleight of hand, she became the aggrieved party. And he, Philip, became a social pariah.

He had constrained his urge to spread the real story in the London clubs, mainly because of his embarrassment at having been green enough to fall for her ploys. At the age of twenty-one, he had been entirely defenseless against her allurements.

For the rest of his years in the navy, there was little opportunity to meet women of any kind, even less to meet young women of good character. Now, here in Bath he found he was still remembered for his youthful folly. His naval record was not widely known; he was just another of dozens of captains who had done their duty. Perhaps there would someday be the occasion to meet the gentry of his new neighborhood, wherever that turned out to be. Maybe he would not be too old to form an attachment.

He retraced his steps to the darkness of a side street, staring up at the stars. Yet scenes from that afternoon swam before his eyes. The comely form of Miss Elliott as she chased the little spaniel, her bonnet blown off, her hair in disarray. Now there was a picture that rivaled the heavens. How could the cold glitter of Orion or Cassiopeia compete with the warm laughter and sparkling smile of a lovely English rose?

Three

Wide awake well before Nell brought her morning chocolate, Rosalind ran over the subjects she might raise today to draw out her grandmother on the cause of her feud with Lady Isiline. Yesterday's social calls yielded many allegations and denunciations of Lady Isiline, but no hints of the original basis for the quarrel. Lady Rotherford had simply refused to speak of her adversary.

Rosalind was determined to ferret out the source of the grudge. If she and Captain Chadwell could bring the old friends back together, then she might see a great deal more of the gentleman. Visions of those future meetings had been the stuff of her dreams.

She snuggled under the covers, searching her memory for recollections of their childhood acquaintanceship. One afternoon the two of them had ridden bareback on a fat pony, she astride behind him and clinging to his jacket. At the time, she had nothing more in mind than to escape from his elder brother. But now the thought of pressing herself to his back brought a warm feeling of satisfaction. And why? Because she wished she could do it again. No longer would it be aboard a swaybacked old pony. She would love to clasp his arms close and press herself to his wide shoulders. The very thought made her warm and tingly.

Where could they go and what could they do? Perhaps ride off to the village of Bradford. Far from Bath's prying eyes, they could sit together at the inn and share a mug of ale. Rosalind had rarely tasted the stuff, but in Chadwell's presence she was sure it would be delicious.

She pulled the coverlet up under her chin and conjured up the picture of him, sitting across the table, his face only inches from hers.

"Miss, yer chocolate's gettin' cold." Nell spoke with the voice of censure.

Rosalind smiled to herself. How the maid would grimace if she knew the direction of the thoughts flitting about under Rosalind's lacey nightcap. Obediently, she straightened up and lifted the cup from its saucer.

"It steams still, Nell." She took a sip of the luke-warm brew, then drained it in one big gulp. "You see, I am about to rise."

Later, following her grandmother's customary morning routine, Rosalind accompanied Lady Rotherford to the Pump Room. The gathering that day seemed to include all of their usual conversationalists. Rosalind settled her grandmother with Lady Marlowe, and brought her a glass of the waters, wrinkling her nose at the sulphury scent of spoiled eggs.

". . . so if he is here in Bath, you can be certain Lady Isiline is also in residence. Why thank you, Rosalind dear." Her grandmother took the glass and leaned close to her circle of friends and spoke in a conspiratorial tone. "I should not be surprised were we to see her this very morn."

"Anne! The very idea!" Lady Marlowe exclaimed. "I declare it has been at least four years since I have seen the woman."

"Oh, indeed, she is here in Bath." Mrs. Winslough nodded furiously, the lace ruffles on her cap waggling up and down in concert with her multiple chins. "I myself had the opportunity to give her the cut direct just yesterday in a shop on the High Street."

Lady Rotherford gave a little gasp.

"When I saw her I turned right around and left the place." Mrs. Winslough's nods grew even more frenetic. "I took my custom next door, and I watched her leave with her footman, whose arms were full of packages."

"Hmmpf! Trying to buy her way into the good graces of the merchants, I suppose. Much good that will do her." Lady Marlowe sputtered with indignation.

"Grandmother, what is the reason you and Lady Isiline quarreled?"

Lady Rotherford frowned at her granddaughter. "I told you last night, I do not ever wish to revisit . . ."

"Quarrel? Quarrel?" Indignation shimmered in Mrs. Winslough's harsh voice. "There was no quarrel. It was entirely one-sided . . ."

"Good morning, ladies. You are all looking in fine fettle today!" Sir Humphrey White struggled over his corpulent middle to make his bow, grabbing the back of Lady Rotherford's chair to steady himself.

"Ah, welcome, Sir Humphrey," Lady Marlowe said. "And what news have you of your granddaughter's confinement?"

Sir Humphrey drew up a chair and settled his

considerable bulk with an audible creaking of his corset. "M'wife writes that the babe is healthy and squalls loud as a flock 'a crows . . ."

Rosalind turned her attention from the conversation to a survey of the well-populated groups of chairs. She noted the presence of Admiral Gladfeller, Mr. Carbaugh, and Lady Melrose, and nodded in their direction. Rosalind's friend Fanny Gilmore sat with a group of companions at the opposite end of the room.

On any other morning, she would have joined Fanny for a refreshing conversation free of the gossip that always occupied the Pump Room habitués. Fanny inhabited the center of a circle of ladies who scorned the usual Bath topics, occupying themselves with literary topics or discussion of plays and concerts.

But this morning, Rosalind had another purpose in mind. Again she peered around the room. It was so difficult to think of which regular attendees were not here. She hoped it was a safe time to meet Captain Chadwell without being seen by those who would find the meeting a prime subject for tittle-tattle, however carefully she and the captain contrived to make their encounter seem accidental.

The thought of seeing his smile again gave her a little shudder of pleasure. Perhaps he might have some progress to report and at the very least they could set up a time for another meeting later in the week.

She listened again to the conversation.

". . . was it the old earl's third or did he have a fourth wife? Old goat had children spread over forty years if a day."

"Excuse me, Grandmother. While you are here, I want to see if my book has arrived. I shall return for you within the hour. May I look for something for you?"

Lady Rotherford waved her hand dismissively. "No, dear. You go along. I will wait right here."

"Thank you. Can I bring anyone another glass?"

"How kind, but we shall be entirely cared for, I assure you. Birks is waiting to attend us." Mrs. Winslough pointed to her uncomplaining companion, who waited patiently a few feet away.

Rosalind stood and gave a little curtsy. "Then I shall wish you all good morning for the moment."

As she hurried from the Pump Room, her heartbeat began to quicken. Her whole countenance felt lighter in anticipation. How silly she was to have such a strong reaction to a clandestine meeting. Of necessity, it could last only a moment or two. But as she hurried toward Bond Street she eagerly searched the pedestrians for his tall figure.

Once inside, Rosalind looked around Barratt's Library, both to find Captain Chadwell and to survey the morning's attendance. She sincerely hoped there was no one here from among her Grandmother's circle. Most of them were comfortably ensconced back in the Pump Room, where they would stay for at least another half hour. But there might be someone who could see her with the captain and find their meeting a matter of potential interest to others.

She wished she had something of substance to report. All she had heard was a catalogue of that lady's many transgressions against an extraordinary variety of persons, all unforgivable, all horrendous, all intolerable. All irrelevant, in Rosalind's view. The original source of the dispute remained a mystery.

In what she hoped was an offhand manner, Rosalind picked up a magazine and ambled across the room. There were entirely too many people on hand this morning, probably because the weather was unusually fine. She tried to appear to be reading the magazine as she moved slowly and peeked up to see if she could locate Captain Chadwell.

She felt as though every eye in the room were focused on her, waiting for her to speak to someone. Perhaps there was an army of little notebooks ready to record her every movement. She shrugged off the feeling of being tracked like a rabbit.

Every face seemed familiar. Had she not seen that gentleman in the old-fashioned wig at the Upper Rooms? Had not that lady in black been at the concert when Madame von Henke sang last week? And certainly the gentleman with the two canes had played whist with her grandmother, more than once.

Oh, this would never do. If Captain Chadwell came, they were sure to be seen talking together. If either Lady Isiline or her grandmother got wind of their objective to instigate a reunion of the two ladies, the task would be spoiled before it really began.

Rosalind stood with her back to the wall, her head bent over a magazine and peeked sideways at the door. She glanced down at the page, read nothing, and stole another look. There was no sign of him, but she felt her heartbeat quicken again, as if Captain Chadwell were near.

She watched the door with such intensity she recoiled in surprise when she heard him speak her name.

"Miss Elliott? Oh, I'm sorry to startle you."

She turned slowly and spoke softly. "Good morning, Captain. I am afraid I know several people here. If we are seen together, tongues will wag. I fear our plan could be ruined before we get started."

"Quite so. By the way, do you always read the *Sporting News*?"

The desire to let her eyes linger on his face nearly overcame her and she felt herself blushing. "I never miss it. Did you learn anything?"

"I have only a long litany of grievances, but some of them might give us a clue."

"Shh. Mrs. Crawford is looking this way." She nodded in the lady's direction, then folded the magazine and placed it on a table. She began to look at a London paper.

"I'm afraid this is not the place for a rendezvous. We might as well be at the Parade," she whispered.

"Can you be outside Sydney Gardens on Thursday at four?" he asked.

"Yes."

The next time she looked up, he was going out through the door.

Hours after her meeting with the captain, Rosalind still felt all astir, her pulse quick, her body tense with some sort of feeling she could only describe as restlessness. She found herself fidgeting, a trait she particularly despised. If her grandmother came into the room and saw Rosalind's fingers wound in her skirts, Lady Rotherford would instantaneously sense Rosalind's disquiet. In order to keep her jittery hands busy, she took a scissors and a sheet of prints from the desk and began to cut around the image of a ruined temple.

After Captain Chadwell left Barratt's a few hours before, she searched for a book she could pretend to have ordered. In her agitated state, nothing appealed to her, but finally, selection in hand, she hurried back to the Pump Room, where Lady Rotherford still chatted merrily with her companions. Rosalind had peered around the room again, fearful that someone might just have arrived after a stop at the circulating library. She was absolutely no good at prevaricating. A lifetime of good behavior had never prepared her for intrigue. A tiny little incident, when passed through three or four sets of wicked lips . . . not only would the plan be ruined, Grandmother would have spasms if she ever heard of Rosalind's meeting with "that man."

She snipped a corner of the design away, then crumpled it and threw the scraps on the fire.

Just as she picked up her scissors again, Jaspers assisted Lady Rotherford into the room and placed her chair at just the proper distance from the fire.

"Thank you, Jaspers. If you could coax Cook into discovering some seed cake, I would have a slice with my tea. Rosalind?"

"Yes, if you please." She smiled, thinking of how Cook baked a fresh seed cake every third day, knowing of Lady Rotherford's partiality. The pantry was never empty.

Jaspers closed the door of the room behind him. Rosalind applied her scissors to another drawing, this time of a Greek urn. "This morning, Grandmother, Mrs. Winslough started to talk about your dispute with Lady Isiline. I do not understand why—"

"No genteel person would ever understand. That woman has the tongue of a venomous serpent. I declare I shall be distraught until she leaves town. Do not try to wheedle me into talking about her. As far as I am concerned, she does not exist."

"But you were the best of friends."

Lady Rotherford's mouth was drawn into a tight knot of displeasure and she turned her head away.

Rosalind breathed a little sigh of relief. If she and Captain Chadwell had been seen, at least no one had rushed to the Pump Room to report it.

"What could have come between you? Perhaps another was envious of your closeness?"

Her questions were met only by silence.

Four

Rosalind grasped her deep blue cloak and turned it inside out. Wearing the gray lining on the outside made it much less noticeable. She pulled a deep poke bonnet from the back of her armoire, a hat she considered a mistake the moment she'd brought it home from the milliner's. She ripped the cluster of silken forget-me-nots from its brim and stripped off the matching blue ribbon. In its place she draped a narrow green cord, tying it beneath her chin instead of in a pert bow at her cheek. She hunted up a pair of black gloves, and went to the looking glass. Beneath the shadow of the deep brim, her face was hardly recognizable. No one would expect to see the usually fashionable Miss Elliott in a deep poke bonnet, enveloped in gray, and wearing mourning gloves.

She tiptoed to Lady Rotherford's door and listened for a moment, content to hear the gentle snores that proved her grandmother enjoyed a restorative nap.

"I am going to call upon Miss Gilmore," she told Jaspers. Please tell Lady Rotherford I shall return in good time to prepare for tonight."

"Very good, miss." Jaspers' tone did not disguise the disapproval he felt for her solitary journey.

Rosalind knew her independent ways disturbed the butler, though not her grandmother, who was lenient to a fault. Jaspers was definitely of the old school. Neither did Jaspers approve of the blue-stocking ways of Miss Gilmore, she suspected.

She was glad for the comfort of her cloak, for the breezes were chilly as she hurried toward the Bridge and the long avenue of Pulteney Street leading to the Sydney Gardens. A group of ladies inspecting a shop across the street paid her no attention, proving the efficacy of her apparel to obscure her usual looks.

The persistence of her thoughts about the person and character of Captain Chadwell bewildered her. It was not only the rapidity of her pace that caused her heart to race as the park came into view. No man in her acquaintance, whether in London or in Bath, had ever absorbed her attention in such an unyielding manner. She tried to discern a simple reason for her fascination with the man, but she could not. Yes, he was handsome and charming, but she knew the unsavory nature of his reputation.

For many years she had attempted to avoid men like him, who apparently had no shame in having compromised a lady. Indeed she had little experience with men of the world, men who flirted and romanced their way through society without regard for strictures against such misbehavior.

If things had been different in her family when she made her first forays into London social circles, perhaps she would have known more about men. Her first Season had been postponed by her father's illness. The next year she was presented at court, but after only a few parties and the tiniest taste of the *ton,* her Season was cut short by his death. She left London, never to return. She nursed her mother for three years, too distracted by Mrs. Elliott's troubles to indulge in more than a few neighborhood assemblies. And once her mother joined her husband in the churchyard at Fosswell Manor, Rosalind left the estate in the hands of the bailiff and came to live with her grandmother in the elegant, if sober, mansion in the Royal Crescent.

Other than her long friendship with Delphine and her occasional visits with Miss Gilmore, she led a quiet life, visiting Lady Rotherford's friends and accompanying any number of elderly ladies and gentlemen to card parties and assemblies.

She actually preferred the company of the older Bath residents to the girls her own age. The young women were mostly concerned with complaining about the tedium of Bath, its dwindling elegance, its dearth of lively entertainment, and the shortage of eligible gentlemen. Bath society, they repeated over and over, had sadly declined. The interesting people, the truly fashionable, and certainly all the attractive young men, went to Brighton or other seaside locations for their amusement. Bath was dull, dreary, and deadly boring.

Nevertheless, in the past three years of Rosalind's residence in the spa city, at least a dozen suitors had sought her favor. It seemed that quite a few of the grandmamas living in Bath had relatives who visited, not a few of whom were gentlemen on the lookout for wives.

But Rosalind rarely gave any more than the merest glimmer of notice. As the sole recipient of a considerable inheritance, she had known such attention since childhood. From the time she was about twelve, when it had become obvious she would probably not have brothers or sisters to share the family wealth, her father had received numerous offers for Rosalind's hand. After his death, the barony and its lands went to a distant cousin. But those were only a fraction of the family holdings. Rosalind inherited Fosswell Manor and all her father's investments, along with many more offers of marriage. She was devoted to caring for her mother, who suffered a protracted decline before dying quietly.

Rosalind considered herself lucky both her father and her mother had refused to arrange an alliance for her. But she sometimes thought it would have been easier if they had. For every man—young or old, wealthy or pockets-to-let, seeking a first wife or a new mama for his motherless children—every one of them knew the approximate size of her income, the extent of her estates, the value of the family jewels, and in which London bank vault they resided.

Even the rare gentleman who tried to court her as he would a young lady of modest means eventually slipped and revealed his knowledge of her financial affairs. Rosalind realized she had grown distrustful and suspicious, even cynical. Her heart never had been deeply involved, but she had sometimes hoped enough to bring on spells of the dismals at the inevitable end of the romance. There had been Charles, an otherwise attractive young man, who allowed himself one too many glasses of champagne and told her of his admiration for her Yorkshire lands. That night Rosalind sobbed into her pillow, desperately sorry his indiscretion caused her to lose trust in the fellow. With Hugh, she had even tried to ignore his questions about her income, to pretend his flattering whispers of endearment were sincere.

All in all Rosalind's prospects for making a love

match seemed nil. She tried not to refine upon the situation and succumb to self-pity. Instead she concentrated on attractive alternatives to marriage and motherhood.

Caution was her byword. For more than twelve months, she had not been tempted to show favor for any man of any age. And now, the least eligible, most inappropriate, improper, and unsuitable man in England was the object of all her attention, conscious and unconscious. It was ridiculous.

Yet her blood flowed warm in her veins, her pulse thudded, and her whole being simply quivered to think of standing beside him, of looking into his deep gray eyes, of hearing his voice.

If only she and Delphine were able to set themselves up in an independent establishment . . . but Delphine had found a man she viewed as ideal. And Rosalind truly wished she could do the same.

Ahead, Captain Chadwell stood just outside the gate of the Gardens. She lowered her eyes again and walked past him. At the watchman's box, she showed her subscriber's ticket and entered, taking the first graveled path to the right, deeper into the gardens until she found a secluded bench surrounded by dense undergrowth. Other than the chirping of birds, it was entirely quiet. Good Lord, she hoped he had recognized her; she had not directly looked at him.

Philip watched her coming from a long way off. Her energetic pace gave her away, the same pace she had set on the way to Barratt's Library. Apart from his instinctive recognition of her willowy figure and purposeful stride, he might not have recognized her in drab gray with a high-crowned, deep-brimmed bonnet shadowing her face.

He sauntered toward the entrance to the Gardens, noticing only a few people nearby. A woman shook her finger in the face of a small child and a chairman slouched against a tree, idly tossing a coin into the air. Across the road, a crossing boy swept up the droppings from a team of horses.

Philip stopped short of the gate to peruse a listing of upcoming attractions at the popular resort. Equestrian feats of astounding agility, remarkable jugglers from the Orient, illuminations of brilliance, rivaling those seen at the peace celebrations in London. All these and many more delights awaited ticket holders for the next evening's performance, where collations of unsurpassed delicacies could be reserved. Excellent service was promised for parties in private boxes.

As he finished the list of culinary delights, he decided a reasonable amount of time had passed. Keeping his steps as unhurried as Miss Elliott's had been rapid, he paid his sixpence entry fee and strolled into the park.

He had chosen the hour of four, and was pleased to see his theory was correct that few people would be on hand. Too early for the evening's attractions and too late for beginning an afternoon's promenade.

He took the path to the right, following Miss Elliott's trail. He found himself energized at the prospect of spending a quarter hour in the company of the lovely young woman. Their two encounters had shown him contrasting attitudes. At Haeffer's, her wide smile and heartfelt request for his help had charmed him. At their brief meeting at Barratt's Library, however, the tension caused by the fear they might be seen had cast a cloud over her lovely countenance.

The path curved and led to a fork ahead. He hoped today Miss Elliott would be more at ease. As he approached the intersection of paths, she stepped out from behind a hedge some distance ahead and waved to him.

Feeling suddenly lighthearted, he strode toward her, unconsciously breaking into a wide smile.

She stood before a bench set into a narrow bower. And for just a moment, she turned her head so that he could see her face, thankfully not frowning with anxiety but wearing an expression of hope.

"Good afternoon, Miss Elliott. Shall we sit?"

"By all means."

They settled side-by-side, turned a little toward each other so that their knees almost touched.

"I hope your efforts with your great-aunt have been more productive than mine with Grandmother. She is resolute in her determination not to speak of the past." She turned her head just a mite and her face disappeared into shadow.

"May I ask you a boorish question? Can you push your bonnet back a little? I feel like I am talking to a faceless hat." As soon as the words escaped his mouth, he was sorry, but she quickly removed the offending apparel, with a rueful laugh.

"Yes, this is a dreadful thing. I fell prey to the wheedling of a Milsom Street milliner a few months ago. She assured me it was all the crack, but ever since, I have been sorry I parted with my money. Nevertheless, if I am to go about town alone, wearing such a concealing chapeau has its advantages."

"Thank you, Miss Elliott. I feel much better now, knowing with whom I am speaking. As for Lady

Isiline, she chooses not to talk about Lady Rotherford. However, I did discern a small point which
might give us an opening into the controversy. The
original disagreement occurred at the card table. I
do not know when or where. Perhaps it was a squabble about gambling debts."

"Well done, Captain. That is a very good hint. But,
oh dear, if it was a charge of cheating, I fear we shall
have great difficulty in effecting a reconciliation."

"Yes, a charge of dishonor could complicate the
situation. I sincerely hope this will not be so. I will
press on in my efforts to learn more."

She smoothed her fingers over the brim of the
bonnet. "And I shall do the same. I cannot believe
either of them would cheat at cards. Both are very
honorable ladies. I am sure it was a small thing that
got magnified again and again as it spread around
the drawing rooms and assemblies."

He tried to keep the scorn out of his voice. "This
city thrives on gossip of all kinds from the most be-
nign to the most spiteful and malicious."

"I myself become quite perplexed by the constant scandal broth in Bath, but then I think about
these poor elderly people, so many in pain and unable to enjoy life. Exchanging news is about the
only activity that gives them pleasure. Most of them
mean no harm."

"You are extremely kind and benevolent, Miss
Elliott."

"I often feel sorry for them, or at least I try to feel
sympathy. But it can be difficult, especially when
someone takes it upon herself to examine the details
of my life as if it were hers to criticize."

"Does this happen often?"

She gave a little laugh. "Indeed, too often. But

never mind. The other day at Mr. Haeffer's we talked about the times we met when we were children. I remembered another incident. One day we tried to escape your brother on the back of a very fat pony. I don't remember why he was chasing us."

"Nor do I, but now that you restore it to my memory, I also remember the pony ride. That fellow lived to a ripe old age, despite the size of his middle."

"And you never had to bring him to Bath for treatment of his joints?"

He laughed out loud. "No, we did not. Just as I think many of the infirmities treated here might be better accommodated in a fellow's home patch."

"How is your eldest brother?"

"I see little of the baron. Get a letter now and then. He has a lady wife, three sons, and two daughters. But he feels the same way about going home to Farreach House as I do. Our father's wife makes every visit a trial. In fact, one of the reasons I am here in Bath is to escape Henrietta."

"Charlotte's mama?"

"Yes. Unlike our childhood habits, my brothers and I agree these days. If our father committed any transgressions in his younger days, he is now being properly and completely punished for them."

"Is she such a termagant?"

"She is the ultimate in self-centered hypocrisy. She fancies herself a woman of great beauty and commands continual accolades from everyone around her." He stopped, thinking how uncharitable he must sound. "I beg your pardon. I should not speak so of my family."

"Oh, I excuse you, Captain." She laughed. "From my gleanings among conversations here in Bath, I imagine that second wives can very much be the source of familial conflict."

"Indeed."

He heard the sound of approaching footsteps and the mumble of several voices. Her face suddenly clouded and she pulled her bonnet back into place.

"Someone seems to be coming our way. Come." He quickly stepped over the bench and tugged her with him through the dense branches of the yews, pressing himself against the trunk of a tree and holding her motionless against him.

He could barely make out the figures that passed them, three persons involved in their own conversation. As they passed, she did not shift an inch but he felt her slight tremble.

He had an unaccountable urge to kiss her as the footsteps receded.

"Thank you." Her whisper held the quaver of fright.

He stifled his impulse and instead stepped back. "I am sorry to have yanked you so suddenly, but I know how concerned you are about being seen with me."

She drew a deep breath. "Captain, I only fear that if we are seen, someone will report to one or both of the ladies and we will never get the two of them together."

The dimness of their spot and the way the branches conspired to keep their bodies close had a strange effect on him. Again he had to fight off the desire to push that bonnet back, clutch her to him, and cover her mouth with his. He fought to keep his breathing steady and normal, then helped her through the shrubbery and back over the bench.

"Do you ride?" he asked, stepping out into the path.

"Yes, I have a horse stabled near the Crescent."

"Can we meet again on Monday, at the crossroads beside the mill?"

"I can be there at one, while Grandmother rests."

"Capital."

"Until Monday, then," she said.

"Until Monday." He watched her shake out her skirts and straighten that absurdly high poke bonnet, then walk briskly back toward the Garden entrance.

He lowered himself to the bench again and ran his hand through his hair, dislodging a twig and several bits of leaves. His behavior had verged on the crude. If he had given into his desire and kissed her, she would have been shocked and offended, and rightly so. What had come over him?

Rosalind wished she could break into a run and flee the Gardens. But she checked her haste in order not to draw attention to herself if she encountered other late-afternoon strollers.

The moments she spent clasped in Captain Chadwell's arms, hiding in the shrubbery beyond the little bench, had been strange. Frightened of discovery and heart pounding with fear, she also felt a pleasure, a sense of delight she had never experienced before. She did not know how to explain her feelings, but she wished their embrace had lasted longer, much longer.

Oh, he was a dangerous fellow indeed. She did not know the exact details of the deeds that branded him a libertine. Her grandmother suggested something scandalous had happened long ago. If, indeed, he was a true rake, he could have taken quite impermissible advantage of her a few minutes ago. Yet he had not.

His actions were protective, not bold and presumptuous. He had behaved quite like a perfect gentleman. The pounding of his pulse she felt with her ear pressed to his chest marked nothing but his concern they might be discovered. He was anxious about her status, her reputation, nothing else.

She encountered no one except a nursemaid with two children as she left the Gardens and continued her long walk home to the Royal Crescent. She knew so little about the captain. Even though they had spent time together as children, his career in the navy began at a very young age when he was sent off as a midshipman. Now, a decade and a half later, he had been a man of the world for a long time.

She was in the dark about the particulars of his life, what ships he served on, where he sailed, what battles he fought. Somewhere in that span of time, he had earned a raffish reputation that still lingered. Her grandmother would be unlikely to enlighten her.

Perhaps she could prod a discussion of his past by the Bath quizzes in the Pump Room. But those ladies, both shrewd and shrews, would take note of her interest and probably find her concern a juicy topic in itself, exactly the kind of gossip she particularly wished to avoid.

Of course she could simply ask him when they met on Monday. What would he make of such a question? Would he think her too forward? He certainly had made it clear how much he despised gossip. The last thing he appeared to want was to become the object of tattlemongers.

Did she have a right to seek the information? The thought of discussing him, of putting into words her feelings, was both worrisome and tempting. Worse, she could trust no one to give her an unbiased view.

She kept her head lowered and made sure her black-gloved hands were in view as she crossed the Pulteney Bridge and took a roundabout route home.

Long walks were among her favorite activities, but usually she enjoyed observing the people in the streets, the parade of sedan chairs and carriages, the facades of the handsome buildings, the wares on display in shop windows. Today she kept her eyes on the pavement and with nothing else to occupy her mind, her thoughts returned to the captain's embrace.

Embrace might not be quite the correct term, she mused. His intentions were not to hold her in his arms, as a lover might, but to keep her hidden and still. Her reaction, the shivery feeling she had felt, the wish his arms would tighten about her—these were the foolish responses of a green girl. To him, it was an act of kindness to shield her, nothing else.

She should be far from a green girl anymore. She had endured the attentions of a number of men, few thinking of her protection. Precisely the opposite, in fact. Their intentions had been only too obvious.

Ah, there was the key. The problem was her loathsome tendency toward contrariness. She reacted to his lack of interest, to his friendly but distant attitude. How very lowering to realize he was not the slightest bit interested in her as the prospective object of his affection. Unlike most of the men she encountered, he had not expressed any but the most offhand compliments. His little bit of teasing had grown out of their long-ago acquaintance, not from the desire to form a closer bond.

If he had been forward in any way, she would have immediately rebuffed him. Instead, he was almost aloof. And contrarily, she had a fascination for him. She was in danger of developing a kind of romantic affection for Captain Philip Chadwell.

The thought made her break her stride and stop, grabbing a convenient railing along the edge of a stoop. Romance? One did not joke about such a word. Where in her head had it come from?

Indulging in romantic ideas about Captain Chadwell was the very last thing she should do!

She walked forward, only a short distance now from home. She refused to be stymied by an idle thought. Or one caused by the overexertion of walking too fast with her eyes on the pavement.

Romance, indeed. Why, she had spent no more than a few minutes in his company since she was about eight years old. What humbug she was succumbing to in her haste to get home and out of this nasty bonnet.

Though it would have been very pleasing if he had kissed her. Just once.

"Rosalind, where have you been? I declare you won't have time to eat before we leave for the Upper Rooms. And look at you. How can you go about as such a dowd? It is that Fanny Gilmore. I don't know why you want to spend your time with her."

Rosalind held her bonnet behind her back and tried to strip off the black gloves while her grandmother dithered. "Have Evers bring me a tray in my room. I will change immediately."

She gave her grandmother a peck on the cheek and hustled up the stairs to her spacious room. She stuffed the gloves in the bonnet and shoved it to the back of her armoire, then flung her cape on the satin slipper chair.

Her sensibilities threatened to engulf her in confusion and turmoil, and she felt on the verge of a good cry. How she wished she could drape herself over the bed and indulge in a spate of tears.

But, she told herself, she had not reached the advanced age of twenty-five without learning to hide her emotions and put a good face on things. Tonight she would have to exchange pleasantries with her friends just as though this afternoon's events had never happened. As if she were just the same as she had been earlier this afternoon when she donned that atrocious high poke bonnet and set off for Sydney Gardens.

Five

"Miss Elliott, please accept my gratitude for the dance. You are a most obliging partner."

At the conclusion of the set, Rosalind allowed herself only a polite smile and a nod of her head. "You are most welcome, Mr. Earnest."

"May I bring you some refreshment? Perhaps a glass of punch?"

"Thank you for your thoughtfulness, but I am quite certain my grandmother will be ready to retire." *Please, let it be so,* Rosalind silently implored. Another minute with Mr. Earnest and she would let out a screech loud enough to perforate the gentility of this evening's gathering at the Upper Rooms. Mr. Earnest, she deduced, endeavored tediously to live up to his name.

"Where is Lady Rotherford? I must return you safely to her."

She looked about the room, finding no trace of her grandmother. "I shall join Mrs. Burton, if you please."

"Could I tempt you to a stroll in the park tomorrow afternoon, Miss Elliott? Or would you prefer a carriage ride in the direction of Bristol?"

"I promised Grandmother I would accompany her to the portraitist tomorrow. In fact I shall have my afternoons taken up with sittings for some time."

"Then I shall look forward to seeing you at the Pump Room and here again next week."

She sank onto a chair, smiled, and nodded as Mr. Earnest greeted Mrs. Burton and slowly backed away.

Mrs. Burton cast an appraising eye on Rosalind. "And how do you do, my dear? I declare, I find Bath lackluster these days. Hardly a whisper of amusing tittle-tattle. Perhaps you and Mr. Earnest might offer us some amiable diversion?" Mrs. Burton raised her dark eyebrows and tipped her face forward so that her several chins formed a series of concentric half-moons below her face.

Rosalind stifled a grin at the comical visage beside her. "I am afraid I shall disappoint you again, Mrs. Burton."

"Had all three of my daughters fired off before they were twenty, miss, and your coming up on five-and-twenty. Methinks you are being too particular. Don't say you're holding out for love, whatever that is. You need a fellow with good consequence."

"How very right you are." Rosalind rearranged the folds of her gown's silver overskirt. The thought of a gentleman's good consequence immediately conjured up the image of Captain Chadwell. Mrs. Burton would no doubt be appalled.

"Your good looks will not last indefinitely. We all thought that Sir William was an ideal match for you. I collect his opinions were the same, was that not so?"

"You are not the first to have been misled about Sir William's interest." Or that his polite demeanor with the ladies masked a propensity for wagering well beyond his means.

"Everyone knew he was looking for a biddable young lady. But I suppose perhaps you prefer a less countrified fellow, someone who might have more elegant tastes." There was an edge to Mrs. Burton's needling tone.

"I think Sir William made an excellent choice in Miss Richardson. Harriet will make a wonderful mother to his children." However much she would like to express her pity for poor Miss Richardson, she limited her observations to the mildest rejoinders, knowing her every remark would be passed from one busy tongue to another before the evening concluded.

"I should not be surprised to hear that she is soon increasing and adding to Sir William's brood."

Where, oh where is Grandmother? If this conversation went on much longer, Rosalind might be tempted to address the subject of pugnacity among the ladies resident in Bath. Certainly she was sitting beside one of the prime examples.

Receiving no response from Rosalind, Mrs. Burton turned to Lady Shawcross. "Have you heard any news, Clemencia?"

Lady Shawcross jerked upright, awakened from a slumping snooze, and grabbed at her teetering plumed turban to set it straight. "News? What news?"

"I say, is there any news of Sir William and his bride?"

Mrs. Burton spoke so loudly that heads all over the room turned her way.

Lady Shawcross fumbled for her fan. "Her mother ain't in Bath. Coming by autumn they say."

Rosalind murmured her intention to find Lady Rotherford and slipped away before Mrs. Burton began a further interrogation. Holding firm to her smile, Rosalind headed for the card room. As suspected, her grandmother was there, frowning at her hand of cards. Another half hour would pass before she was ready to leave.

Rosalind fled to the ladies' retiring room, pleased to find a quiet refuge. She sat before a looking glass and pretended to pin up a few stray locks. How tiresome it was to be quizzed over and over again about her private affairs, as though being young and unmarried meant every acquaintance had the right to make judgments on every aspect of her life.

She was indeed five-and-twenty and never had experienced more than a passing fondness for any of her dozens of suitors. In general, they were a passel of fortune hunters most interested in her annual income, which was substantial, and her estates, which had enjoyed several decades of excellent management by her father and his stewards before they came to her. She sought a man who would love her for herself, who would look beyond the handsome account balances and beneath her facade of conventional good looks and customary good manners.

She liked to expand her mind, to study distant lands and ancient peoples. Unlike most of the young women she knew, Rosalind read voraciously: newspapers, treatises of learned societies, essays by eminent scholars, and even an occasional novel. Indeed, she had a passion for knowledge.

Other than her growing friendship with Fanny Gilmore, Rosalind pursued her bookish activities alone. She had learned at an early age that most persons were suspicious of intellectual curiosity. Though she had been lucky enough to attend a school where Latin was part of the curriculum, the students' skill in needlework and deportment was emphasized over the pitiable efforts of Miss Bright-stone, a meek little spinster who attempted to instruct her charges in a few Latin texts easily obtained in translation.

Not that Rosalind aspired to become a bluestocking. In truth she wanted nothing more than a husband to cherish and children to treasure. Since this future depended upon finding the ideal match, and since no eligible prospects seemed to come her way, she led a tame existence of relative freedom to read, study, and amuse herself.

Usually, evenings here at the Assembly Rooms were pleasant enough. But tonight, tonight was different. Was it the lingering effect of Delphine's letter?

Or was the cause of her disquiet related to her meetings with Captain Chadwell? Just the thought of comparing the looks and bearing of Philip Chadwell with Mr. Earnest, for example, made her giggle out loud.

On Monday, Rosalind found Lady Rotherford in her boudoir, applying a little tortoiseshell brush to Pip's silky ears.

"Grandmother, can you manage the sittings this afternoon with Evers and Nell accompanying you?"

"I suppose I could, but I thought you enjoyed watching Mr. Haeffer paint, at least since we arranged to have our appointments on days other than those on which he has that dreadful child on hand. Have you made other plans?"

"I thought I might take advantage of the sunshine to exercise Cinnamon. We have not been out for more than a week."

Lady Rotherford sighed. "Take care you do not catch a chill. The winds are high."

"Thank you, Grandmother. I shall be vigilant." She gave the little spaniel a pat. "You behave yourself, Pip."

When she changed her clothes, Rosalind rejected her newest riding ensemble for today's meeting with Captain Chadwell. Its military style and matching shako was au courant, but somehow inappropriate for keeping company with someone who had served the Crown in reality. Instead she donned her simple velvet skirt of deep blue and its jacket of a lighter shade.

As she dressed, she wondered how her heartbeat could continually sustain the jolting it received every time she thought of Captain Chadwell. It happened so frequently she was amazed that she still drew breath. In the middle of a meal, halfway through practicing a sonata on the pianoforte, while escorting her grandmother on morning calls, whenever she thought of the captain, her pulse leapt to swift hammering in the space of an instant. She felt quite silly, blushing at nothing, when he had only expressed his most gentlemanly concerns about her. Nothing in his manner should cause her to act so foolishly. But here she was, trying on hat after hat, wondering which would best meet his approval.

The high poke bonnet was not a candidate. Not only would it catch the wind and probably carry her off her horse, but there was really no point in attempting concealment. Cinnamon, a coppery bright bay with a distinctive white blaze, could not be disguised.

At last she settled on a small black hat pinned tightly to her curls.

She stopped by the kitchen and snapped off a chunk from the sugar cone in the pantry. "Ye be spoilin' that horse," Cook said, as she never failed to do.

And Rosalind's response was the custom as well. "It's her version of seed cake, you know. If Grandmother and I can indulge, so can she."

With a merry wave, she let herself into the narrow garden which connected to the street leading to the mews.

Within the hour, Rosalind neared the mill. She had given the mare her head for a brisk canter over the flat stretch atop the Lansdowne hill, then turned westward to wend her way indirectly to the mill. Grandmother would disapprove if she knew Rosalind rode unaccompanied, but Rosalind loved the feeling of independence she had without a groom trailing along behind her. And putting the mare to a gallop helped her work off some of the tensions she felt in advance of seeing the captain. She turned her mind to the delights of the wind in her face and the power she felt as the mare's muscles surged beneath her.

She approached the mill by the road from Charlecombe after circling around on her long ride. She walked Cinnamon, cooling her after the energetic gallop.

Captain Chadwell joined her from a side road near the millpond. "Good afternoon, Miss Elliott. Lovely mare."

"Thank you. She is Cinnamon, a particular pet of mine."

"Just a touch of bite in her spice, right?"

"Precisely. Which way should we head?" Cinnamon danced around, eager for more action.

"I doubt this hack can keep up with your mare, but shall we take a bit of a gallop?"

"Then let us go back toward the open fields."

They turned their horses and, after making way for a cartload of hay, rode side by side under a canopy of trees coming into full summer leaf.

"Miss Elliott, I can not tell you how the beauty of the countryside improves when one has been many years away."

"Your years at sea gave you a greater appreciation of the forest?"

"Yes. I love the sea, the wind and waves, the vastness of the sky. But I also value the oaks and beeches, the yellow flowers, the blackbirds. Earlier this afternoon I watched some lambs playing tag, a sight once so familiar I paid no attention. Today seeing the sheep was a joy, as though I had met up with an old friend. As it was when I saw you at the artist's house."

Rosalind felt her heart soar to new heights. "Your words are well chosen, Captain. You flatter me and at the same time tease me about my failure to grasp the beauties of the countryside."

"Neither was my intention. If I wanted to flatter you I would talk about your renowned good looks or your fine seat and hands on that mare. If I chose to tease you, Rosalind, I would poke at you for wasting time with so many dowagers and doddering graybeards at the Pump Room."

"And I should remind you, Philip, that someday you will be very happy to have lived long enough to take your place there without the carping of younger men who have yet to experience the vicissitudes of old age."

He laughed and nodded. "There you would have the right of it."

As they neared the edge of the trees, the sunshine seemed to beckon them forward.

"What do you say to taking them out?" She turned Cinnamon's head toward the open field.

"Lead on!"

At her signal, the mare minced into a rolling canter, then faster as she heard the other horse beside her.

Rosalind leaned into the rocking of the motion of the horse and laughed out loud. She threw a look at Captain Chadwell. This is how he would have looked on the deck of a ship, the wind in his face, his hair spraying back from his forehead. Or would he always have worn one of those humped bicorn hats she saw on naval officers? No matter, he must have inspired his men with his self-confidence and strength.

Cinnamon's easy stride indeed outpaced the captain's mount. As they approached the trees, Rosalind swung her mare to the right in a wide arc, heading back to their starting point.

She pulled up at a crossroads, where the right turn led directly to Lansdowne and the straight path wound down a longer route to meet the main road into Bath. The captain's horse had slowed his pace and arrived less promptly, blowing a bit.

Captain Chadwell laughed. "I suspect this fellow hasn't had such a run in quite a while. I shall have to walk him back to the livery by the long road.

Should not have him arriving all lathered and winded. When shall we meet again?"

"Perhaps I shall have something to report next week. I tried to rouse Grandmother to talk about her old card partners, but it was futile. She caught on immediately."

"I have had no luck either. Shall we try meeting at Mr. Haeffer's? No one will be surprised to see us there. I can wait for you in the garden when you and Lady Rotherford bring the pups for their next sitting."

"I suppose that will be possible." Rosalind took her reins in one hand and tried to repin her hat more securely.

"Here, let me help you."

They brought the horses to a stop and he reached over to touch her hair. But the horses did not care to be so close and sidled away.

"Sorry." He urged his mount nearer, but again Cinnamon stepped away.

Rosalind grinned. "Never mind. Cinnamon is just being a good chaperon. Grandmother must have had a talk with her."

"I do not want to see you lose your hat."

"I think it will stay on now." She scrunched the pins more firmly into the black felt. "Thank you for trying."

"My pleasure, indeed. When is your next appointment?"

"We are due there on Tuesday next at two in the afternoon."

"Then I shall see you in the daisies."

"Au revoir, Captain." She turned the mare onto the Lansdowne road. She felt his gaze on her back, but did not turn and wave. If the horses had cooperated she would have been more than ready to lean into his arms again. Who knew where that might have led, for she simply craved his touch. More the fool she was!

Six

Philip's hack plodded up the hill on a loose rein. The beast was not about to run away with him, at least not until it neared its home ground. Which allowed him the time to reflect on his admiration for Miss Elliott. A young lady as lovely and amiable as Rosalind must have many admirers. The fact she had not married was surprising. Not even Aunt Isiline, who described Lady Rotherford in such vituperative terms, had naught but agreeable words to say about her granddaughter, Miss Elliott. Perhaps if their plotting resulted in a reunion of Aunt Izzy and Lady Rotherford, he might investigate Rosalind's attitudes about marriage. Why had she never accepted a proposal? Certainly she must have had opportunities. He shifted in the saddle. What business was it of his?

The probable reunion—blast if he had not completely forgotten to tell Rosalind the one further bit of intelligence he had. That the card game at which the original quarrel had taken place was at Lady Vincent's house. It had completely slipped his mind.

His dash of laughter caused the horse to swivel its ears, but otherwise make no change in its gait. Had he really forgotten or was he stretching out the plan in order to increase the number of his meetings with Miss Elliott? Or, had he been too eagerly plotting the next rendezvous with Rosalind to remember his report? Whichever turn of mind it had been, the result was the same. Funny how convoluted his thought process had become where she was concerned.

Other than seeing Rosalind, he really had no desire to stay longer than necessary in Bath. There were several more schools to visit on Charlotte's behalf. Then they had either to settle the feud or consider their goal an impossible task.

At the top of the hill, he reined up for a moment and surveyed the view. Spread below was an irregular pattern of woods and fields, clumps of buildings hugging the busy London-to-Bath Road. In the center was the village of Batheaston, where the track he now followed joined the main route before crossing the Avon. From this distance, it looked serene, presided over by a square bell tower, like a bucolic painting by an old master.

As he watched, the Royal Mail came into view, bringing its cargo of letters, newspapers, packages, and passengers to the city more eager to receive them than any other he could imagine. Especially Charlotte, who wanted to see pictures of the dresses chosen by her namesake Princess Charlotte for her trousseau. To please his half sister, he hoped the much-anticipated ladies' magazines were on that very coach.

Rosalind backed away from Popsy after straightening her ribbon. "Good dog. Stay there."

The spaniels posed on a blue cushion in front of a dark red velvet drapery in Jason Haeffer's studio.

After several sessions, perhaps they were learning the routine.

"Mr. Haeffer," Lady Rotherford said, "I do wish you would allow me just one little peek at your canvas."

From beside his tall easel, Mr. Haeffer raised a hand in protest. "You know the policy, my lady. Not until I am finished."

"But I am so anxious to see my darlings' portrait."

"Grandmother, I will await you downstairs." Rosalind left the two humans restating the identical exchange they recited at every sitting, while the dogs looked back and forth from one to the other speaker.

She paused in Haeffer's deserted drawing room to rearrange her hair. Her pulse increased in a now-familiar design. She could see pink rapidly color her cheeks and, if she was not mistaken, brighten her eyes. There was not a thing she could do about it, though she looked more like a girl about to make her curtsy to the Queen than a woman trying to do a favor for her grandmother. She shrugged and walked through the library to the garden steps.

Captain Chadwell was waiting for her beside a vine-covered arbor. "How are things in the studio?"

He looked his usual calm and deliberate self, unmarked by the kind of silly sensibility she suffered. "Pip and Popsy are better behaved than Grandmother. She is trying to convince Mr. Haeffer to let her look at the portrait today. Of course he refuses."

He waved her to a seat on the wooden bench while he remained standing with one elbow propped on the trellis. "If he allowed such previews, the man would never finish, I suppose."

Rosalind pulled a bough of the rose vine closer

and sniffed a shell pink bud. "Precisely his feelings, I am sure."

On the opposite wall of the garden a collection of cages housed brightly colored canaries whose warbling tinged the air with melody. Rosalind closed her eyes and let the magic of the moment drift over her. With the warmth of the sunny afternoon, the low-pitched buzzing of bees, and the scent of the blossoms, her thoughts strayed far from the ordinary environs of a Bath garden.

She could almost imagine Captain Chadwell and herself alone in a remote garden where he could cut her a basket of flowers and present them with a kiss. A lovely soft kiss . . . she opened her eyes to find him gazing into her face. "Forgive me, I think I am a little carried away by the singing canaries." She could feel her blush deepening.

"Their song can be almost intoxicating. From time to time we had them on board ship. Some of the men grew quite attached to their birds."

She drew a deep breath and tried to throw off her dreamy feeling. "Tell me, have you made any progress?"

"Lady Isiline dropped only one more little hint. The disagreement began at Lady Vincent's house, at a card party, as we already knew."

Rosalind let the rose swing back into place. "Lady Vincent. I believe she died shortly after I came here to live. Grandmother was devastated to lose her, but I remember hearing lots of talk about all her unpaid gambling debts. Some people were most put out when her daughter announced that she would honor only her mother's bills from tradesmen, not markers from her supposedly friendly companions."

"She would not have gotten away with dismissing

gaming debts of honor in the navy. Or in a London club."

"No, I suppose not. Did you get any hint of dishonesty on anyone's part? That is my biggest worry."

"No, nothing like that. At least, not yet."

Rosalind smiled in relief. "I shall see if Grandmother will talk about Lady Vincent. If she will not, perhaps I can approach Mrs. Winslough or Lady Marlowe."

"Strategy is the key to winning battles."

"How is Charlotte?"

"Oh, yes, my other battle. I am actually developing some sympathy for the child. She is lonely. I am the youngest of father's first family, and we are all long gone from Farreach House. She has no one to play with. She said her mother does not allow her to associate with the tenants' families, so she has developed all sorts of little irritating methods of gaining attention. I feel sorry for her."

"Then I suspect she is anticipating school with some pleasure."

"I am afraid not. She manages to defy all discipline at home but she knows things will be different at school."

Rosalind felt sad for the girl at the same time she deplored the child's rude behavior.

Captain Chadwell sat down beside Rosalind. "I do not recall you had any brothers or sisters back when our families met from time to time."

"Yes, there is only me, though my parents often took me to play with other children in the neighborhood. Also, I had a vivid imagination. My mother read stories to me, and I learned to read at an early age. I acted out the stories with my dolls. And I had a lovely big dollhouse."

"So you had a happy childhood."

"I did."

He stared into the distance. "I was in constant trouble. Everything my older brothers did was blamed on me."

"And if you started in the navy at age twelve, your actual childhood was rather short."

"Not too short for me to believe what everyone thought of me. I enjoyed being a demon."

"So why are you surprised that your half sister is such a handful?"

"Touché! Miss Elliott, you are indeed perceptive."

"Oh, just observant, I think."

They laughed at the same time. Rosalind turned toward him and their eyes met. The laughter faded and they sat still, the moment lengthening. Rosalind felt sure he could hear the pounding of her heart.

His eyes, ringed by long lashes as dark as his hair, were clear gray with green highlights, like the sea on a stormy day when the sun bursts through the clouds. His cheeks were sun-darkened, his lips slightly parted.

Her heart raced out of control at the thought he might kiss her. The tension between them grew stronger, like the lull just before a great storm breaks. She wanted to lose herself in the gale, wanted it to sweep over her, wanted to drown in his arms.

He did not move, their eyes locked.

Rosalind shook herself into reality. She almost lurched against him, caught her balance and stood, drawing a deep, throbbing breath. "I must go back . . ."

Captain Chadwell looked momentarily stunned, then nipped to attention, straight and tall beside her, his face impassive. Again the voices of canaries sounded through the soft spring air. The sun shone brightly; no hint of a storm threatened.

He broke a small rose from the vine and twirled it in his fingers. "Of course. When can we meet again?"

"Friday? In the country?"

"I will meet you at the mill, where we met before."

"Yes. I will be there."

Rosalind rushed back into the house. They had not touched, though she felt he had covered her face with burning kisses. She paused in the hall at the foot of the stairs to catch her breath and attempt to soothe the ache deep within her.

"Grandmother, I have a request you might find a little strange."

"A strange request? Now you fascinate me, my dear."

"If I were to have my dollhouse sent here to Bath, could we put it in one of the third-floor rooms?"

"Your dollhouse? Whatever would you want with that?"

"I was looking at some toys in a shop a few days ago, and I remembered in what disarray I left my poor little family. I thought I might at least put up some new curtains for them and sew them some clothes."

"Good heavens, Rosalind. I know that netting a bag or embroidering a cushion has never been your favorite activity. Do you really want to make doll clothes?"

"Perhaps I could manage something very small better than I did those sleeves I tried to decorate. The dolls' costumes were very shabby the last time I looked."

"I have no objection. If having your dollhouse to adorn would make you happy, then by all means write for it."

"Thank you, Grandmother, dear. I told you my request was strange. I will write to Fosswell Manor before I decide I really have lost my mind."

Rosalind had not dared to mention Lady Charlotte to her grandmother. What the captain had said had touched her heart. Yes, her own childhood had been a happy one, but there had been times she knew loneliness. She had a bit of an idea of how Charlotte might feel. Someday, when the ladies were reconciled, perhaps Charlotte would enjoy playing with her dollhouse.

Just another excuse to be with Captain Chadwell is it not, Rosalind, you devious one?

Seven

In the brightly lit anteroom before the concert, Rosalind felt as though she existed in a partial trance. One part of her smiled and chatted with friends, commented upon Lady Fleming's new spangled slippers, remarked on the considerable improvement in Mr. Farwell's complexion, listened to the latest *on-dits* from London about the royal wedding. Another part of her, the innermost source of her feelings and thoughts, remained totally disinengaged from the evening's activities.

The buzz of conversation filled her ears, yet she hardly heard what was being said. The chandeliers, the object of much admiration, glittered with light, yet she barely saw the finery surrounding her. The glass of punch she held sparkled with pink pinpoints of light, yet its taste made no impression.

In her heart, she felt only the wonder of a new sensation. She had not come to terms with this fresh notion of special regard for Captain Chadwell. The implications of her discovery remained to be explored. The entire effect was one of heightened consciousness and downright enchantment. On the morrow, she knew she needed to sort through the meaning of her strange discovery; for now, she floated on a cushion of

happiness undisturbed by importunate questions
she could not answer.

Eventually, their party moved toward the rows of
chairs, and she sat between Lady Rotherford and
Miss Jones. Just as the orchestra began to tune, she
heard her grandmother gasp aloud, jolting her into
concern.

"Are you unwell?" Rosalind whispered.

"Just look over there," Lady Rotherford said.
"That woman has had the gall to come here."

Rosalind saw only that Captain Chadwell stood at
the opposite end of the row in front of them. He
was dressed in evening clothes, dark and elegantly
handsome, but unsmiling.

"I cannot comprehend what brings her to this
gathering when everyone in Bath spurns her company."

Rosalind automatically reached out to pat her
grandmother's hand but kept her eyes on the captain as he seated a lady of advanced years and took
his place beside her. Even in his chair, she could see
the top of his head, his chestnut hair glinting in the
light.

"I never thought she would have the nerve!"
Lady Rotherford hissed.

No one in the hall seemed disturbed by the appearance of Lady Isiline and her nephew, as far as
Rosalind could tell. No one except her grandmother
and herself. And for entirely different reasons.

Rosalind leaned close. "Do not upset yourself,
Grandmother. The last thing you want is for anyone
to think her arrival is bothersome to you."

"But I cannot stay . . ."

"Nonsense. You could not give her the satisfaction

of seeing you withdraw! Here now, the music is about to start."

Lady Rotherford grasped Rosalind's hand tightly as the concert began and she pressed her lace handkerchief to her lips.

Even through their gloves, Rosalind could feel her grandmother's quaking, but as the music began the tremors faded. Again Rosalind looked toward the captain's position and caught sight of the back of his head until some lady in a wide turban changed position and blocked the view.

Even so, Rosalind knew his presence as a palpable caress. She sensed the blush on her cheeks, her breathing rapid and shallow, her toes curling inside her shoes. The music sounded like melodies from the heavens.

Time seemed to stand still. The only reality was the thump of her heart.

Eventually she broke out of her reverie at the applause that marked the interval. Lady Rotherford got to her feet, apparently fortified for the interval as the audience members moved about and sought refreshments.

"Do not look over there, Rosalind. Pretend you do not see them. But mark anyone who deigns to speak to her."

Rosalind could not help positioning herself so that she could see him, his height rivaling some of the ladies' waving plumes. She suspected he could not see her through the bustle of the crowd. Just as well, for she feared if they came near each other, everyone would instantaneously know of her *tendre* for him, a feeling she would have to suppress before they met again.

Several ladies gathered around her grandmother,

all talking at once, mostly about Lady Isiline's arrival.
Gradually the group made its way to the refreshment
room and Rosalind lagged behind, conflicted about
what to do. She wondered if the captain wore
breeches and silk stockings as most of the men did,
then felt a blush as she realized how very much she
would like to see his legs. She felt a little flush come
to her cheeks. At no previous time had she ever en-
tertained such a thought!

From the rest of his physique, she very much assumed his calves would be shapely, for his thighs
were muscular . . . what was she thinking? If she uttered such thoughts aloud, every lady in this entire
assemblage would shriek in dismay. She opened
her fan and set a little breeze on her heated cheeks.

What would he see if he caught sight of her? Her
gown of pale azure silk was modestly cut at the
bodice but had almost no sleeves to alter the lines
of her shoulders or hide her slender arms. The
hem of the dress was richly trimmed with ruched
borders of silver and white, but somehow she did
not expect him to pay much attention to the bottom of her skirt. Nell had dressed her hair,
anchoring a hothouse rose and a tangle of ribbons
in the knot atop her golden curls.

As he had this afternoon, his eyes would probably
linger on her face. She fanned herself more briskly
and moved along to catch up with her grandmother's party.

"Good evening, Miss Elliott."

She snapped her fan shut and turned slowly, unable to clear completely the silly grin she knew she
wore.

"Captain Chadwell. I did not anticipate seeing
you here."

"Nor did I intend to come. Aunt Isiline was un-expectedly invited by an old acquaintance."

Their gazes locked for a moment. He looked so very different tonight in his formal wear, austere and imposing. The sun-darkened skin, the lively gray eyes were the same.

For an instant he lifted an eyebrow and gave a quick grin before bowing and moving on. She stood rooted to the place, watching him step through the throng in the anteroom. She had the tiniest glimpse of his breeches and silk stockings. Very fine calves indeed.

Recovering her purposes, she hurried to her grandmother's side, surprised the conversation did not center on Lady Isiline. Someone had arrived with the news of a grandson's betrothal, as far as she could ascertain. The family of the young bride-to-be was being thoroughly examined for distant connections and incipient conversational value. No one mentioned her brief encounter with Captain Chadwell; apparently it had gone unnoticed.

Rosalind was surprised to see a tinge of melancholy on her grandmother's face. The lady hardly participated in the chatter, and left her teacup on the table without ever raising it to her lips. Moving to her side as they started back to their seats, Rosalind tucked her grandmother's hand over her arm.

She kept her voice low and private. "What was said about Lady Isiline?"

Lady Rotherford shrugged. "She was little dis-cussed. All it has done is to give me the headache."

"Do you wish to have me call for the chairs?"

"Of course not. As you said earlier, I shall not give that snake the satisfaction of seeing me leave. She no doubt would consider herself able to drive me off. That I could never abide. So, migraine or not, I shall stay."

Not until the second half of the concert had begun did Rosalind dare to steal a peek in the direction of Captain Chadwell. He was in his place. The lady who previously had spoiled her line of sight appeared to droop into a little nap, and Rosalind caught a clearer view of his profile. His entire demeanor seemed in sharp contrast with the elderly gentlemen she saw daily and with the town-bred and dandified young men who often sought her favor. The captain was rugged and strong, a man who would be most at home in a uniform or astride a horse, but who filled out a formal jacket with a strongly masculine beauty. She shivered a little, as she thought of sitting beside him this very afternoon.

As she brushed out her hair, Rosalind worried about Lady Rotherford's distress in seeing her declared enemy, even across the room. Though Rosalind wished to give way to her dreams about Captain Chadwell, she could not avoid seeing the pain in her grandmother's eyes. Along with the venom with which Lady Rotherford had expressed her feelings about the other woman, there was another side to her grandmother's anguish. Regret and sorrow, not loathing.

Once in her nightclothes, Rosalind went to her grandmother's boudoir.

"Please, Grandmother, tell me what happened on that night when you were playing cards at Lady Vincent's."

"Ah, Rosalind, you are nothing if not persistent.

I thought I had made it clear the matter is not a suitable topic for discussion."

Rosalind did not want to mention her suspicion that Lady Rotherford suffered from sorrow. "Tonight I saw the look on Lady Isiline's face. She looked very sad. I thought for a moment she might come over and speak to you."

Actually just the opposite was true. If Lady Isiline's glare had been a sword, Lady Rotherford would have been run through. But Rosalind thought she could detect a softening of her grandmother's stance. "How did it all come about, this falling-out between old friends?"

Lady Rotherford crumpled to the bed and passed her hand over her forehead.

"It was all a long time ago. But I remember every detail as though it were only this morning. We were at cards, yes. Prudence, that is Lady Vincent, called for more refreshments. She was pouring spirits that evening. Perhaps she wanted to ruin our concentration and shadow our judgment for she had been losing badly."

Rosalind sat beside her grandmother and rubbed her shoulder.

Lady Rotherford drew in a deep breath. "Someone asked me about Rotherford, how we had met, if it was arranged by our parents. We talked about marriage. Isiline said she heard Rotherford offered for me at the behest of his father, who had worked out the details with my father. Of course, that was not so, and I said so. I told her she was mistaken. She said I had a discerning memory. At first we all laughed.

"Then Prudence said she heard I had a great many admirers in my day. Lady Isiline said we all did, didn't we? I agreed and it would have ended

there. Except then Isiline said she had more suitors
than any girl in London in 1762. I admit I was a little hurt by that, for I remember having more
suitors than she did. But I let it go. Then within a
day or two, all Bath was gabbling about how Isiline
and I had been great rivals in our London Seasons.
And somehow the story became a *cause célèbre*.

"For weeks, we both tried to stop it, thinking the
story had been started by Mrs. Pettibone, who refused to admit to her deafness and often confused
others' conversations. But I began to hear how Isiline was voicing subtle insults, then outright
untruths, then colossal lies about me."

Lady Rotherford took the square of linen Rosalind
offered to wipe her tears.

"I was crushed. Lady Vincent strongly defended
me and Mrs. Pettibone tried also. Everywhere we
went everyone was talking. And they have talked
ever since."

Rosalind was not surprised the quarrel had begun
so simply.

"You mean you and Lady Isiline did not go arm
in arm to the Pump Room and dispel everyone's
suspicions? Did you not show your affection for
each other?"

"Of course we did. But eventually I could not
bear hearing about the things she said. For a time,
I stayed away from everyone. Then she left town
and everyone called on me, to tell me I had been
slandered and to declare their devotion. I heard
many more stories about the awful things Isiline
said. Until tonight I haven't laid eyes on her."

"You never wrote to her, Grandmother?'

"Lady Vincent had a last note from Isiline with

such scathing comments about me that she refused to show it to me."

"What happened to Lady Vincent?" Rosalind asked.

"She passed on the very next year." Lady Rotherford drew in a long, shuddering breath. "She was my true friend, but she died without ever paying her card debts. Not that it mattered . . ." Her voice dwindled away.

Rosalind wanted to shake her grandmother's shoulders. Was it not obvious that Lady Vincent had fueled the fires of a minor and laughable disagreement, fanning the flames until the conflagration consumed a close friendship and also burned away the lady's debts? Instead Rosalind wrapped her arms around her grandmother.

"How very painful this was for you. But perhaps Lady Vincent exaggerated some of the things Lady Isiline said."

"Oh no, Prudence Vincent would never have done that. At least, I never believed she would."

"But Isiline never told these lies to your face?"

Lady Rotherford turned away, her eyes bright with tears. "I never had a better friend than Isiline before this all happened. I admit it all sounds excessively foolish when I tell you the story."

"Not foolish, Grandmother. Just very sad. And perhaps the result of someone's resentment against the happiness you and Isiline once found in each other's company."

"Perhaps so, my dear. But it is far too late now to do anything about it."

Rosalind chose not to disagree, for the moment. A remedy for the break could come later, after Lady Rotherford had thought a little more about how much she missed her old friend. If Philip had any hint that Lady Isiline felt the same way, they could take the next step.

She helped Lady Rotherford into bed and blew out the candle. "Good night, Grandmother."

Back in her bedchamber, Rosalind sat on the bed and hugged her knees to her chest. So she had the story to tell Captain Chadwell. How could she wait for another two days to pass before she could ride out to meet him? How handsome he had looked tonight. . .how romantic, how tantalizing. And how foolish she was.

Rosalind had found her grandmother quite distracted during the next morning's activities. At the Pump Room Lady Rotherford avoided conversation about last night. She sat with two ladies who had not even been at the concert.

Rosalind promenaded the length of the room with Fanny Gilmore. "I know I can count on your discretion. I need your advice."

"Of course, my dear." Fanny was not the kind of person to indulge in gossip, even in the Pump Room.

Rosalind explained the mission she shared with Captain Chadwell to reunite their elderly relatives.

"And now you are telling me that Captain Chadwell is the man of your dreams?"

"No!" Rosalind almost sputtered in her surprise. How did Fanny know?

"It would not be a secret to anyone who hears you repeat his name. Your voice carries your feelings in its melody. Your eyes are sparkling, your cheeks bright, and you obviously are about to jump out of your skin with excitement."

"Oh, Fanny, you mean I am so terribly obvious?"

"You are to me. And probably would be to some of these old tabbies here in the Pump Room. They are much more expert at divining people's secrets than I am."

"This is dreadful. Until Grandmother and Lady Isiline are bosom bows once more, no one must know Captain Chadwell and I have even met, much less will do so again on Monday. I cannot possibly let our conniving become known or Grandmother will never give in and see her old friend. She is the most stubborn . . ."

"Can I do something that brings them all together? And necessitates you and the adorable captain meeting at my rooms?"

"Fanny, you are the very best of friends. I am truly obliged to you and in your debt forever."

"I only ask you to take caution, Rosalind. You have long been vigilant, perhaps overly so, about gentlemen who seek your favor. This is the very first time I have suspected you of losing your heart. What do you know about Captain Chadwell?"

"Very little, to be sure. Our families were friendly when we were children, but he went off to the navy. I had not seen him for at least a dozen years until a few days ago."

"And what of his associations with women? A man of his looks and breeding could not have gone unnoticed in society."

"Grandmother says he is a libertine. He committed some awful indiscretion, but that was many years ago. I wish I knew more, but . . ." Rosalind paused.

"Then I can do you another service, my dear. I dislike the gabble-mongering that is Bath's *raison d'être*, but I do have my connections. Some of them swim in a river of twaddle that rivals the Avon."

"Fanny, I shall ever be in your debt."

"Indeed you will not. All I ask is that you spend your time with the captain assessing his character. Knowing you have made the effort is all the repayment I require. Tell me here on Tuesday if my offer meets his approval."

Eight

"Your dollhouse has arrived, Miss Elliott." The butler met her at the door and took her pelisse. "Lady Rotherford had it carried up to the third floor."

"Thank you, Jaspers. I shall go there directly."

By the time she hurried to the top of the house, Rosalind breathed hard but her curiosity grew with every step. She hadn't seen the dollhouse for several years, and she was surprised at her eagerness to see just how it looked after its journey from Fosswell Manor.

The house, at least four feet wide and easily as tall, stood in the center of the room on a large table. The front was vaguely Palladian with a neoclassical doorway and five windows across the top floor. Five rooms opened to the rear, the parlor and the dining room on the sides of the ground floor entrance hall, and three rooms above. The furnishings from each room had been boxed and sat to the side, leaving the dollhouse empty.

Memories flooded through Rosalind as she peeked into the empty rooms. Her mother had sewn the curtains that hung in the bedchambers out of scraps of ivory silk left from one of her own gowns. Rosalind remembered how lovely Mama had looked in that dress, and the tears welled into her eyes. Mama's beauty had matched her kindness and her caring for her daughter.

Rosalind sank into a chair and wiped her eyes. When she told Captain Chadwell her childhood had been ideal, she had been understating the case. The only thing that would have improved her early years, perhaps, was a little brother or sister to share in her good fortune. Mama and Papa must have been disappointed not to have additional babies, though no hint of their disappointment had ever reached her attention. But then, like all children, Rosalind knew she had given little thought to what her parents' life was like beyond the nursery.

Rosalind did not dare allow herself to think of having children of her own someday. She had put that thought away long ago, for to acquire a family meant first finding a husband. And there was the rub! Why could she not have made that choice before she realized what attracted her suitors? Other girls married men for whom their marriage portions had been of great importance. Why did she find a man's interest in her fortune to be so prickly?

Because she was no fool. Rosalind straightened her spine and held her head high. There were too many instances of men who married only for the money, who cared little for their wives. Once a woman married, everything she had came under the control of her husband. She heard of men who even supported their mistresses with money from their wives. Not to mention paying off gambling debts or acquiring a string of racing horses.

She refused to allow herself to refine upon the situation anymore. She would not marry a fortune hunter and that was that.

Rosalind blinked away the last of her tears and reached for the large box of furnishings for the house. Someone had carefully wrapped each piece in tissue paper. She would have to write immediately and thank the staff at Fosswell Manor for their care in preparing the dollhouse for transport.

Gently she unwrapped the little chairs and the table for the dining room. The chandelier with its tiny chain and the miniature candlesticks for the sideboard were next, followed by a little set of china. She felt as though she had uncovered the contents of a treasure chest. Each cherished piece was more precious than the last, and her memories washed over her with renewed sentimental attachment.

Halfway through the box she came to the dolls, and here was where her efforts at rejuvenation were most needed. The little mother and father both wore clothes that had seen better days. When she used to reenact the scenes from her favorite books, it seemed her little hands had been less than spotless. She set the two dolls aside.

"I'll have you in better outfits very soon, little ones." She spoke out loud, but somehow, talking to her dolls seemed entirely natural.

When she unwrapped the next piece, the tears leapt back into her eyes. The infant lay in a tiny wooden cradle, wrapped in rather dingy white flannel, with arms outstretched. How endearing was the look on the baby's face as she reached out for someone to lift her from her bed. Rosalind grabbed for her handkerchief and blew her nose. She was being incredibly silly, she knew, but the baby that lay on her lap, no bigger than her thumb, represented a beloved promise, a dream still eluding her. How many years ago had she snuggled this baby into the bed?

Many years ago, before so many illusions had been shattered, so many dreams dashed.

Rosalind, get a hold of yourself. You are submitting to childish sentimentality and exaggerated sensibilities.

She gritted her teeth, set the baby in an empty room, and reached into the box for another tissue-wrapped item. When she saw it was the little girl, she could hold back her tears no longer.

She did not know how many moments had passed before she heard the clicking of the dogs' feet on the wooden floor of the hall and the tapping of her grandmother's cane on the stairs. Lady Rotherford was coming up to see the dollhouse. And she would find Rosalind awash in tears.

She used a little of the tissue paper to dry her cheeks, but she knew her reddened eyes would betray her anyway. Popsy slid across the bare floor and put her paws on Rosalind's knees. "You rascal. Grandmother, can I help you?"

Lady Rotherford answered from the stairs. "No thank you, my dear. I am coming, but slowly."

Rosalind went out to meet her grandmother. "The dollhouse is much more wonderful than I remembered." She took Lady Rotherford's arm while the old lady caught her breath.

Near the dollhouse, the dogs snuffled in the tissue paper and sniffed around the edge of the box. Rosalind managed a little laugh. "Don't you wonder what they find so fascinating about odors we hardly even notice?"

Lady Rotherford seated herself where Rosalind had been sitting, heaving a big sigh. "Those stairs get steeper every year. Now as to the way my little darlings touch their noses to everything under the sun, I think it is done only to confound me. They have to assert their superiority somehow and they know I will never get down on my knees to see what they are doing. You don't think they let any spiders get into that box, do you?"

"I am sure they did not." As Rosalind brought over another chair, Popsy jumped into Lady Rotherford's lap. Rosalind scooped up Pip and sat hugging him to her chest. "Look how carefully they wrapped everything."

"Why look at this darling baby doll. Very adorable . . ." Lady Rotherford picked up the crib and smiled. She looked up at Rosalind and abruptly stopped. "Why, Rosalind, you have been crying."

"Just some childhood memories making me into a silly watering pot, that is all."

"Yes, I suppose you are thinking of your darling mama. I do not know why she had to be taken from us at such a young age."

"Oh, Grandmother, do not cry too." Rosalind's eyes again overflowed with tears as her grandmother reached for her handkerchief.

Popsy hopped up on Grandmother's lap and tried to lick away her tears.

Lady Rotherford hugged the dog. "Oh, you precious little beast! I do adore you, but you are not my dear Georgiana, are you, my pet. Nor my wonderful George, the finest of husbands."

Rosalind bit back a sob. "I do not mean to upset you. The dollhouse just brought back so many memories. I am sorry you have been caught up in my reminiscences."

Pip tried to join Popsy in Grandmother's arms,

and Rosalind went to them. Her hug encased both spaniels as well as her grandmother.

Lady Rotherford tried to laugh. "What a sight we must make."

Rosalind found herself laughing too. "I will call for Nell to bring up some dry hankies."

"And perhaps a pot of tea. All this sensibility makes me very thirsty."

Heavy clouds hung over the hills above Bath when Rosalind looked out the window of her bedroom on the morning of her next meeting with Captain Chadwell. Now that she had most of the story from her grandmother she was eager to tell the captain. They had made no provision if rain spoiled the prospect for riding out that afternoon.

The fact that her hands trembled just thinking about him had nothing to do with the importance of the meeting. Absolutely nothing.

She watched the skies on her trips to and from the Pump Room with her grandmother. Once home, she tried to concentrate on a novel, but stole frequent glances out the window. Certainly the sky lightened moment by moment as she turned the pages, mostly unread.

Grandmother yawned over her copy of *La Belle Assemblee.* "I shall go up a little earlier than usual for my rest today. It looks like it may be fine later and I have a bit of shopping to do. Mrs. Winslough said several drapers had new stock. Will you accompany me, Rosalind?"

"If it clears, I thought I would take Cinnamon out again. She needs the exercise. The other day she seemed excessively frisky from too much time in her stall. But if I return by three, will there be time enough?"

Lady Rotherford stood and the dogs dashed to her side, anticipating her attention. "If you are not here by then, I will have Nell come with me. Do you have any particular needs if I find the new goods valuable?"

"I can think of nothing. But perhaps, while I am riding, I will change my mind."

When her grandmother left with the spaniels, Rosalind went to the window and looked out over the broad sloping lawn before the Royal Crescent. The clouds thinned to the point where the sun would break through any moment. Her heart lifted. She would see Captain Chadwell in two hours. With a last smile at the brightening sky, she skipped upstairs to change.

After taking Cinnamon for a quick gallop in the fields, Rosalind slowed her pace. She was a bit early and walking the mare allowed Rosalind to build up her excitement and her defenses as well. Remember, she cautioned herself, he has given you no grounds to think he wants to be anything but your friend. And coconspirator, of course. Nothing should have caused you to assume he feels more. Except the moments they had spent staring into each other's eyes. The way he held her in Sydney Gardens. Do not be a ninny, imagining things that were not there!

She should be very cautious. She had never let her emotions run away with her before, and the temptation to do so now had to be damped down. Yet the depth of her feelings surprised her, after many hours of considering the situation from every possible perspective.

Of course she had no idea whether he returned her feelings. Yes, he had been solicitous and cooperative and respectful. She was certain he held her in high regard. But did he see her as a desirable woman? Her only clue was what a wise woman had once told her. People you know well are likely to return familiar feelings. If you like a person, he will probably like you.

When she rounded a bend, she saw the captain standing beside his horse, letting the animal drink from the river above the mill run. All her caution fled and she gave in to a full smile.

His face broke into a wide grin, and her heart leaped in her breast. Perhaps it answered the question she had been asking herself. Did he care about her as more than a fellow schemer? His smile said he probably did.

He wrapped his reins around a branch and came up to Cinnamon, reaching out to lift Rosalind off the saddle.

She leaned forward into his arms and he helped her to the ground. He steadied her for an instant and she had to keep herself from pressing against his chest.

"Your mare looks fine this afternoon." He broke the tension by leading Cinnamon to a point beside his mount and letting her drink. Then he took both sets of reins and led the horses along the road beside the mill. A boy came out to relieve him of the horses.

"I'll loose them saddles, sir. My ma be inside."

"I've arranged for some refreshments for us while we speak, Miss Elliott."

"Thank you." She preceded him into a cozy sitting room. Until she stood near the fire, Rosalind did not realize how chilly it was outside despite the bright sunlight.

The miller's wife curtsied to Rosalind and directed her to a bench beside the fire. Captain Chadwell sat down facing her.

"A lovely day for an outing," he said.

"Indeed," she replied, suddenly tongue-tied in his presence.

The miller's wife brought them glasses of cider. "Would you rather have tea, miss?"

"No, this will do nicely."

The woman left, closing the door behind her.

"I took the liberty of arranging a place for us to be seated out of the wind." Captain Chadwell said.

"Very thoughtful of you." And away from prying eyes, she thought.

"What have you learned?"

"My grandmother confessed all. As we both suspected, the original disagreement was minor. Lady Vincent was probably the villainess. She had some large debts to Grandmother, perhaps also to Lady Isiline." Rosalind took a sip of her cider.

"The ladies played deep?"

"So it would seem." Rosalind gave him the details of her grandmother's story.

He stared into the fire, nodding from time to time. When she finished her account, he began to laugh. "What in blazes caused them to argue about which of them was the Season's diamond after fifty years? You mean that was all they quarreled about?"

Rosalind could not help laughing a little herself. "It sounds absurd, does it not?"

"Absurd and so very unnecessary, so very foolish."

"I think it was abetted by many others. As I pointed

out to Grandmother, other ladies may have been quite envious of their close friendship."

His laughter subsided into a wide grin. "And the one with the gambling debts never paid?"

"So it seems. By breaking up the friends, benefiting from their tiny disagreements, apparently Lady Vincent kept her purse closed." She leaned toward him. "The question now is how we can bring them together. I truly believe my grandmother would end the feud if presented with the opportunity."

"I believe we will have to take the initiative. Can I tell Lady Isiline that Lady Rotherford desires a rapprochement?"

"Indeed, though I do not think we should expect either of them to apologize. From what Grandmother said, neither was really at fault. Harmless remarks were turned into major insults by other people."

He stood and stirred the coals. "But how can we bring them together without a passel of gabble-mongers to witness their reconciliation? In case the cessation of hostilities does not go well, they should not have an audience."

"My friend Fanny Gilmore has offered her good offices. If you agree, we can meet at her house and try to end the hostilities."

He sat beside her on the bench and took her hand. Rosalind's pulse pounded and she gazed into his eyes. She had every confidence he would kiss her and she smiled, wanting him to hurry.

"You are both clever and resourceful, my Rosalind." Slowly he leaned toward her and she raised her face to his, longing for the touch of his lips.

He moved deliberately as if giving her every chance to pull away. She did not move, urging him with all her soul to persist. No! To hasten. The tension built within her until she heard herself give a tiny whimper.

He covered the remaining inches between them immediately. His lips were soft and gentle at first. With one hand he tightly clasped her and with the other he caressed the back of her neck, finally pressing her more tightly against him.

As she slid her arm around him, he whispered her name, again capturing her mouth, this time with insistent pressure, stealing her breath away. She arched against his chest, a strange warm throbbing deep within her. What was this mystifying ache she felt?

He rubbed his thumb along the line of her jaw, the touch of velvet. She ran her fingers into his hair and heard his answering sigh, tantalizing in its promise. She felt as though she were melting, losing all sense of reality. Nothing mattered but his mouth on hers, her body tight against his.

The very second they pulled apart, she wanted to be back in his arms. But he got up and walked across the room.

"I beg your pardon, Miss Elliott."

"No, I am—" Her face was hot and flushed, her pulse pounding.

"The fault is entirely mine. He shook his head in dismay, frowning. "I had no right to . . . I am sorry—"

"No, please." She forced herself under control.

"You must think I am . . ." His voice faded.

She drew a long, deep breath. "Look here, Captain Chadwell. I am not a chit just out of the schoolroom. I do not ordinarily indulge in private meetings with gentlemen nor do I welcome their embraces. But I am not outraged, nor am I forever stained because we kissed." She could hardly believe she had the nerve to utter those words. She tried to mask her real wish that he hadn't stopped. "Can we simply say this little interlude was a foolish error? For both of us?"

"Thank you, Miss Elliott. Again you are most charitable. Be assured I will not slip again."

Oh, but I hope you will! She almost said the words aloud.

She stood and went to the door, looking back as she went outside. The little room was beautiful to her now, warm and sheltering. The high-backed bench looked inviting instead of crude and unadorned. She pressed the image into her mind—the place he had kissed her.

Without further conversation, they found the lad with the horses, and Captain Chadwell cinched up her saddle. She waited for him to lift her onto Cinnamon's back, but he allowed the boy to toss her up. What a disappointment, she thought, wishing for just one more moment in his arms.

"When do you wish to meet with Miss Gilmore? Would Tuesday afternoon be possible?"

"I shall be there. What is her direction again?"

"Number 20 Barton Street. Thank you, boy, and *au revoir*, Captain."

She turned Cinnamon's head toward the path and was quickly out of sight around the curve in the road.

At last she drew a deep and wracking breath. She had been sorry when he broke off the kiss. *My stars, if he had chosen to undress me, I would not have stopped him.* Rosalind shivered though she did not feel chilly.

She urged the mare to a canter. She felt as wild as the wind.

* * *

Philip drew in a lungful of fresh air as he went down the front steps of Miss Foster's Ladies' Seminary. An hour spent in the hothouse atmosphere of the reception room, listening to the deadly dull prosing of the headmistress almost caused his brain to turn to stone. Miss Foster's scrawny figure and stern visage convinced him that Charlotte would be miserable in her custody. The child was prone to whining; she did not need further instruction in the art of complaining. That she had learned well at her mother's knee.

He headed down the hill, determined to wipe from his mind the thought of his stepmother. Henrietta was younger than he was. She had snared his newly widowed father despite the opposition of the entire family, before his father had time to see through her artifices to the bitchy shrew she was.

Despite the warmth of the day, he shuddered at the memory of Henrietta's carping combined with her flirtatious manner and insistence on being the center of everyone's attention. Little wonder that his father claimed deafness and a variety of debilitating infirmities in the last few years.

Henrietta was in every way inferior to Miss Elliott. In looks, in companionability, in . . . what in the deuce was he doing, letting thoughts of Rosalind invade his head again?

Had he not promised himself he would set aside her image in his brain? After he kissed her at the miller's house, he had pledged to himself to put her out of his mind. That ill-considered kiss . . . how had he let himself do it? It was also the kiss he wanted to renew whenever his thoughts strayed to

Miss Elliott, which they threatened to do so often he had taken a bottle of his contraband cognac to his bedchamber.

He chafed at the duties that tied him here to Bath when he could have been out roaming the countryside in search of the modest estate he wanted to buy. He could blame no one but himself. He had offered to escort his great-aunt here and even to bring Charlotte to find a school. At the time, he had thought himself very clever indeed, to separate the child from her mother. Charlotte, after all, was his half sister and if she continued to use her mother as a model for behavior, she would bring nothing but unhappiness to herself as well as the rest of the family.

But it seemed that finding a decent school for a female was not just paying some establishment to enroll her. So far he had visited three schools and had found three versions of female incivility and unattractiveness in charge of each. Why couldn't there be a place which simply tried to bring out the best in a girl rather than drill her in rules, regulations, and strictures that were sure to emphasize whatever bad qualities she already had?

He turned away from the street leading to his residence and strode toward the outskirts of the town. He was not ready to confront Lady Isiline and Charlotte with the bad tidings about Miss Foster. Now where had the charming and intelligent Miss Elliott acquired her education?

No! Miss Elliott again! Why did his mind insist on revisiting forbidden territory? She might be uncomfortable in his presence. Despite her reassurances at the miller's, perhaps she had taken offense after all. Had she gone home and realized how boldly he had grabbed her, how audaciously he had held her close and kissed her? Once she reflected upon his behavior, she might have been revolted to think of how he had used her.

Well, he was not a drawing room kind of man. He had been more at home in that miller's house than in the perfumed drawing rooms of Bath. He belonged out in the open, preferably on the sea. And yet his thoughts strayed again to Miss Elliott, where he would most like to see her . . . in her chamber preparing to come into his arms, clad in a night-rail of fine white lawn, lifting her arms to take the pins from her hair. . . .

Blast it all! How could he stop these devilish thoughts? He stopped and turned, setting a course for home. There was only one answer. Get those two ladies back together, find Charlotte a place in no-matter-how-unsuitable a school—as long as it was fashionable—and get himself away, far away from Miss Rosalind Elliott.

Nine

Rosalind tried to interest her grandmother in Fanny's collection of Roman coins. "And these were found in a well. Do you think that people made wishes to the gods of the waters and threw coins to them?" She spread them on a round table at the center of her drawing room.

Anne, Lady Rotherford, patted her granddaughter's hand. "I am sure they did. Perhaps we should wish on these and toss them back where they came from. We may need the gods' assistance to break through that stubborn woman's obstinate brainbox."

"Now, Grandmother, you promised to be the soul of charity and compassion."

Fanny Gilmore brought a small damaged sculpture for them to examine. "If you will pardon my intervening in a matter which is none of my affair, I suggest we not assume Lady Isiline will be obdurate. She may be anxious to apologize."

Lady Rotherford nodded slowly. "So I must provide her with the opportunity to say her piece."

"Yes," Rosalind said. "Without making her more aggrieved than she already is."

"I know that she will never admit she started everything. I shall have to take the blame." Lady

Rotherford wore a look of suffering as she fingered the statue.

Fanny spread wide her hands, as if in appeal. "That would be a sign of true nobility, Lady Rotherford. A sign of true quality."

Rosalind agreed. "You would not regret asking her pardon. I suspect she, if confronted with such graciousness, will do the same."

"Hmmpf. We shall see." Lady Rotherford handed the statue back to Miss Gilmore. "Was this a little god or someone's child?"

"No one knows. But the experts say it is more than a thousand years old." Miss Gilmore replaced it in a velvet-lined box.

Rosalind went to the window and watched Captain Chadwell assisting his great-aunt out of the chair. He wore the same dark blue coat she had seen before. She remembered how it felt when she had placed her hands on his shoulders and around his neck.

She shook off the recollection. "They are arriving below," she said in a voice that was hardly more than a croak.

Lady Rotherford's face was set in an unyielding mask. Rosalind hurried to give her a little hug. "Smile, Grandmother. We are all desirous of a happy conclusion to this meeting. Once, you and Lady Isiline were inseparable friends."

"As I am only too aware, my dear."

The footman entered and announced the visitors. "Lady Isiline Aldercote and Captain Chadwell."

"How nice to see you," Miss Gilmore said, going to her new guests and directing them into the room.

Captain Chadwell made his bow and Lady Isiline nodded silently to Miss Gilmore.

"We were just admiring a few of my ancient treasures, some Roman coins and a little statue found near here. Of course you know Lady Rotherford and her granddaughter Miss Elliott."

Lady Isiline's mute visage was as grim as Lady Rotherford's. They eyed one another in silence.

The captain made his second bow. "Good afternoon, Lady Rotherford, Miss Elliott. I am pleased to see you again."

Lady Rotherford, saying nothing, stared at Lady Isiline, who returned the honor. Rosalind fought to find an opening gambit for the conversation but found nothing. How stupid not to have foreseen the difficulty in getting through the initial pleasantries.

Fortunately Philip seemed capable of speech. "May I inquire how the portrait of your spaniels is proceeding?"

After a painful pause, Rosalind stepped forward. "Why, quite well, I believe. And what of Lady Charlotte's sittings?"

He looked toward his great aunt, then back at Rosalind. "I believe Mr. Haeffer is nearly finished. Just one more sitting, is that not correct, Aunt Isiline?"

Lady Isiline nodded, not taking her eyes off Lady Rotherford.

"Perhaps you would like to see the coins," Miss Gilmore interjected. "Some of them appear to date from the time of Claudius, but we do not recognize all of the emperors' images. Pick them up and look closely."

Philip and Rosalind found themselves side by side, nearly touching as they reached for the coins. Quickly, they both snatched their hands back.

Miss Gilmore kept up her efforts. "You will see

the amounts stamped on the backs, though some are very worn."

Rosalind picked up a coin and pitched her voice lower, near to a whisper. "This material looks like copper, not gold."

Captain Chadwell followed her lead, his voice so low that both she and Miss Gilmore moved even closer. Rosalind actually felt her hair brush his shoulder. "And this one must be silver, though it is very dark in color."

Rosalind stole a glance at the two old ladies who stood silently staring at one another.

Miss Gilmore whispered too. "Thought to be a silver denarius, old enough to have been brought with Julius Caesar."

Rosalind felt the tension in the room like a heavy pressure on her chest, crushing out the air. Was it the apprehension about what the ladies would do? Or the nearness of Captain Chadwell?

"The Roman version of our penny. Or rather we might say, pennies are our modern version of Roman denarii . . ."

Rosalind hardly listened to Fanny but she strained to hear any scrap of conversation between Lady Isiline and her grandmother. For long moments there was no sound from them, but at last Lady Rotherford spoke.

"I do not know how you do, Isiline, but I am too old to stand here all afternoon. Pray, let us be seated."

"My aches and pains are so numerous I no longer keep track of which ones occur in the morning, afternoon, or evening." Lady Isiline plomped herself down in a chair with the swishing sound of silk on silk. "I came to Bath to see a new doctor but I find him as quackish as all the others."

Rosalind stole another glance; the two former friends sat about five feet apart.

"I rely on Dr. Bevis," her grandmother said. "But I declare he gives me the same powders and drops he prescribed a dozen years ago."

Rosalind directed her attention back to her companions at the round table. "Shall we tiptoe out and leave them alone?"

"I'll lead the way." Captain Chadwell eased toward the door and quietly slipped into the hall.

"Do you have your same bad hip?"

Rosalind heard one of the ladies slide her chair a little closer to the other.

"Both hips. And my back. Sometimes I hardly can climb out of bed . . ."

Rosalind followed Fanny out. Miss Gilmore motioned them into the library at the back of her house, closing the door behind them.

"Whew! For a moment there I thought neither of them would say a word." Rosalind sat on the edge of a chair.

Miss Gilmore poured three glasses of sherry and handed them around. "I think we have successfully broken the ice, my friends."

"Thanks to your good offices." Captain Chadwell raised his glass in acknowledgment. "I am sure I speak for Miss Elliott as well when I express our gratitude to you."

"Indeed," Rosalind murmured. She felt much better now, but a tinge of the pressure remained, shortening her breath and causing her heart to race. No matter how many times in the last week she had tried to tell herself that Philip Chadwell was entirely the wrong kind of man to esteem, no matter how many nights she pounded her pillows to wipe away the wicked thoughts that interfered with her slumber, no matter how many ways she attempted to divert her interest in him, she could not quell her treacherous feelings. Now that she sat only an arm's length away from him, how could she pretend she had not lost her heart?

That evening, silence spread across the Upper Rooms like a wave sweeping across the beach. When every eye in the assembly was trained upon them standing in the entrance, Lady Isiline and Lady Rotherford walked arm-in-arm into the room. They progressed only a few feet before the chatter broke out again at twice the volume of before.

Philip offered his arm to Miss Elliott and followed in the ladies' wake into the dreaded den of societal decorum, stultifying propriety, and idle tedium. He could hardly believe he had consented to come here, this bastion of all he despised about so-called polite society. But when the happily reunited old friends suggested the escapade, he could not bear to extinguish their pleasure by refusing his participation.

All around them, conversation buzzed as the fans fluttered. The Master of Ceremonies fussed over Lady Isiline and Lady Rotherford like the obsequious courtier he was, bowing and scraping so many times Philip wondered that he did not succumb to seasickness.

At his side, however, Rosalind seemed all delight and approval as she watched. The bright candlelight set her eyes aglow and sparkled off the jewels at her ears. He knew her satisfaction was sincere.

Unlike his cynical view, her outlook was unjaded by a sour estimation of these people. She saw them as friends and family, peculiar though some were. He saw them as utter parasites, most of them of no use whatsoever to the operation or improvement of the world.

Rosalind's face was alight with satisfaction. "Look. Everyone can perceive their happiness. What a wonderful reconciliation, quite victorious."

"They owe it all to you."

"How kind of you to say so. But your role was equal to mine, and Fanny managed all of us at the crucial moment, did she not? I am sorry she is not on hand to observe the triumph."

In Philip's opinion, Fanny's rejection of regular attendance at the Assembly Rooms several nights a week was testament to her good sense. Rosalind's look of joy, however, made him keep his thoughts to himself.

Slowly the ladies progressed through the ante-room and into the ballroom, surrounded by persons all talking at once. Philip was surprised to be approached himself.

"Good evening, Captain, it is about time you showed yourself to one and all." The speaker was an elderly gentleman, leaning on two sticks. He wore a wig in the style of the last century, and though his body was spare of fat, his bulbous nose gave him the overall impression of weightiness.

Philip let go of Miss Elliott's arm and made his bow, searching his mind for the gentleman's name. "Your servant, sir."

"I see the old tabbies have made up. Keep the town talking for another few days, they will." He turned to Rosalind. "And Miss Elliott, pleased to see you in the best of looks tonight."

She curtsied with the sweetest of smiles. "Admiral, you always try to turn my head with your flattery."

"I believe it has been a dozen years since I have seen you, Admiral Gladfeller." The admiral had been one of his only defenders when his unfortunate affair with Lady DeMuth was discovered. If it had not been for Gladfeller, Philip's career in the navy might have ended just as he began to come into his own. The admiral's support had followed him all of his career, and Philip owed him a great deal. What a surprise to find him here.

Rosalind touched his sleeve. "I shall join my friend Miss Pettibone, Captain, and leave you and the admiral to renew your friendship."

Before Philip could say a word, she flashed a smile at the admiral and set off in the direction of a dark-haired young lady in pale green.

Admiral Gladfeller watched her walk across the floor. "That is a fine young woman, that Miss Elliott. Now come into the card room and out of this racket so I can hear what you have to tell me. It is not often I get to talk to my boys anymore."

Philip followed the gentleman's slow steps into the nearly empty card room and sat down across a table.

"Tell me of your family," Philip began.

The old admiral took a wheezing breath and gazed into the distance. "My wife is here in Bath with me . . ."

Fully an hour passed before they began to run out of new subject matter. Philip stopped just short of discussing his own future, still protective of his undisclosed wealth and his private plan to acquire an estate near the coast.

"I hope to see a good bit more of you, my boy," the admiral said. "My wife would be pleased to have you call upon her in the coming days, once she is past tonight's indisposition. Indeed, I ought to be getting home to see how she fares. And you ought to be charming the ladies in the ballroom, not lurking here with the gamesters."

"I shall look forward to seeing Mrs. Gladfeller." Philip only now noticed the game room had filled up with players and onlookers. All tables but their corner spot were well occupied.

The admiral got carefully to his feet and propped himself erect with his canes. "Ah, my boy, growing old and feeble is not for the faint of heart."

Philip walked beside him to the door and saw the admiral stowed into his sedan chair. "I shall see you very soon, sir."

When the old gentleman had been borne away, Philip went into the ballroom where a dance set was just forming. For the moment he was content to scan the crowd and find Miss Elliott, who took her place beside a dandified fellow in the formation in the center of the floor. The music started and he watched her graceful movements turning and swaying, then whisking down the line to the opposite end. He tapped his toe in time to the music and realized he had known the steps to this country dance since he was a youngster.

When the musicians finished with a flourish and the dancers moved toward the edges of the room, Philip moved quickly to Rosalind's side, neatly separating her from her erstwhile partner.

"Excuse me, Miss Elliott, for deserting you—"

"I was delighted you and the admiral knew one another. I sometimes think he longs for companionship from others than those who concern themselves primarily with their ailments. I am certain he found his time with you to be more rejuvenating than a gallon of Bath water."

"Is that supposed to be a compliment or an insult?"

She laughed and introduced him to the gentleman who lingered beside her. "May I present Mr. Earnest, who spends part of the year in Bath with his mother. Mr. Earnest, this is Captain Chadwell, the grandnephew of Lady Rotherford's friend."

Philip wasted little time exchanging pleasantries. After a perfunctory bow, he addressed himself directly to Rosalind.

"May I escort you to the refreshment room, Miss Elliott? I believe our relatives are holding forth over the tea tables."

"Yes, I look forward to a little cool drink myself. Again, Mr. Earnest, I thank you for the dance."

She slipped her hand beneath Philip's arm, and honored him with a dazzling smile.

As he suspected, Lady Isiline and Lady Rotherford were surrounded by old friends and, in Isiline's case, not a few former adversaries. Everyone seemed in fine fettle this evening, spouting the warmest of felicitations to one another, smiling and babbling as though three or four years of choosing sides, furthering grudges, and spreading cruel falsehoods had never existed.

Without disturbing the tangle of plumed turbans and feathered caps, he guided Miss Elliott to the perimeter of the room. He left her for a moment and returned with two cups of what appeared to be lemonade. "I am not sure exactly what this concoction is made of, but it is icy and wet, qualities which recommend it to me whatever its taste."

"I quite agree." Rosalind took a sip, then another. "Delicious. I believe that lemon is correct."

Philip would have swigged down the entire contents in one gulp, but stopped with a moderate swallow. This was Bath, after all, and his every move reflected upon Lady Isiline's consequence. He had no idea how much of his tattered reputation remained in the lexicon of current gossip, and he did not plan to find out. In another few days, he would be far way, he hoped.

But for the time being, his companion was a young lady of the highest character, a young lady of whom he had grown fond. Perhaps excessively fond.

She sipped her punch and watched the ladies across the room, a little smile turning up the corners of her lovely mouth. How he wished he had earned her respect instead of showing himself to be a man of impulse, unable to restrain his urge to kiss her in a most unsuitable environment. Could he ever restore her trust? Their mission had resulted in complete success. There was no further excuse for them to meet. He would miss those stolen moments together, not just miss her soft lips, but her humor and intelligence.

"I feel much revived, Captain. I believe we will not be too late for the final set if we return to the dancing."

"I am at your disposal, Miss Elliott. I cannot claim any expertise in the ballroom, but I believe I once learned a few of the old dances. Shall we give it a try?"

Philip could not believe his own ears. Hearing himself offering to dance? But how could he aban-

don her to men like Earnest, poor specimens unworthy of claiming her time or attention?

They joined another country dance with music
he found familiar but could not name. He felt a
little dazed as though the lemonade had been
laced with gin. How much wine had he drunk with
the admiral? Nothing near what his capacity had
been only a few months ago.

He was not quite certain how he recalled the
steps or even if he was turning in the correct direction, but Miss Elliott seemed to be on hand at all
the right moments, her hand light in his, her
cheeks pink and her eyes bright.

Their first dance led into another, this one ne-
cessitating holding tight to her hand as they weaved
in and out, around other couples, ducking under
bridges made of raised arms. Philip found himself
laughing out loud, engrossed in keeping track of
the order of the figures.

When the music finally came to a stop and he finished with a low bow to her deep curtsy, he still
could not keep the smile from his face.

"You dance well, Captain Chadwell. I think you
must have had weekly practice on the decks of your
ship."

The thought made him laugh again. "Drill we
did indeed, but I fear the steps were far less rhyth-
mic and more like scrambling up the rigging."

Two young ladies, barely seventeen or eighteen,
both dressed in maidenly white gowns, passed by
them.

Rosalind leaned close and whispered in his ear.
"Fifty years from tonight, do you think they might
argue about who had the most dances with the
handsomest gentlemen?"

Philip pressed his hand to his mouth to keep from laughing out loud. "No doubt they will scratch each other's eyes out. But I predict they will eventually be reconciled by their grand nephew and granddaughter, who will enjoy the conspiracy more than they ought."

"Oh my! I admit I have excessively enjoyed our conspiracy."

"Now we will have to think up a new excuse to meet."

She spoke in a very soft voice. "I can think of several excellent excuses, Captain."

He looked into her sparkling blue eyes. This indeed was all the excuse he needed. If they had been alone, he could not have resisted taking her into his arms. But he had to be content with simply smiling at her and receiving her glowing smile in return.

The hour of eleven was almost at hand and the ballroom emptied gradually. By the time he had overseen the comfort of the ladies in their chairs and sent them on their way, Philip found himself whistling a little. By all that was sacred, he had actually enjoyed himself. Instead of being bored and cross, he felt energized and cheerful.

Miss Elliott's high spirits had infected him with a very strange malady indeed.

Ten

Rosalind looked out the window once more at the morning's gray skies. She could not see what people were wearing. Was it warm enough for a light spencer or did she need a warmer pelisse? Summer was at hand, but the breezes were still cool and rain threatened. The leaves on the trees were quiet, though, and without the wind perhaps she could opt for the spencer, for it was exactly the color of her feelings today, as rosy as Grandmother's drawing room walls.

She loved the bonnet that matched it, with its ruched lining and bunch of short white feathers on the crown. She peered into the looking glass, pleased to note the natural color in her cheeks, no pinching needed. If she sat in Lady Rotherford's drawing room, she would look like a permanent part of the decor. The thought made her giggle out loud, and caused Nell to start in surprise.

"Are you laughing, Miss Rosalind? Or did you see a spider?"

"A spider? Is there a spider in my room?"

"I hain't seen one, but you sounded a bit put out."

"No, not at all, Nell. I am quite cheery this morning. I thought I might be lost to view if I wore this rose jacket around this house. I am the same color as the walls and the furniture."

Nell shrugged and went back to stirring the grate.

Rosalind gathered up her gloves and reticule and went downstairs to await her grandmother. Rosalind rarely wore any shade of pink. Her late mother had dressed her in rosy shades and after her death, Rosalind had shunned the color as too much of a reminder. Then, when she moved to Bath, Lady Rotherford's house was such a temple of roses and pinks, Rosalind maintained her aversion, until she found the soft wool of this spencer and could not resist its shade so reminiscent of a blossoming crab apple. Her embrace of the color only proved how correctly her grandmother judged the flattering nature of the hue.

She wanted to look her very best this morning in the Pump Room. Everyone would be talking about last night's assembly and how Lady Rotherford and Lady Isiline had mended the breach in their old friendship.

Though her apparel hardly mattered. There was not a soul among the usual denizens of the morning session who would care what she wore. She dressed today for only one set of eyes. Captain Chadwell's eyes, the eyes that last night had crinkled with pleasure again and again throughout the evening. No matter how pointless, how futile, she wanted to look her best. She knew his kiss had been only a whim, a mistake, no matter how much she treasured the moment.

Rosalind wanted him to care for her so deeply he would be as forever changed as she was. If she could have him as her husband, she would jump at the chance. But he had made it very clear his intentions were to set up a bachelor's establishment far from Bath, far from London, away from society altogether.

However, if she had her way, he would never forget her. After all the men who had pursued her, he was one who seemed to have no interest in escorting her to the altar. Life had its twists and turns. She could have predicted that in a contrary way, if she were ever to fall in love, it would be with someone entirely uninterested in her as a wife.

His purpose in coming to Bath was almost over. When he left, he would carry away part of her heart.

The hall mirror revealed a sad expression on her face, quite contrary to the one she had worn in her bedchamber. And now a few pinches of her cheeks were definitely needed to bring them back into bloom.

Perhaps Captain Chadwell would come along to the Pump Room this morning with Lady Isiline. If so, Rosalind was determined he would see only her cheeriest side.

The Pump Room was precisely as she had anticipated it would be. The trill of eager voices complimented Lady Rotherford on last evening's appearance with her good friend Lady Isiline. How lovely, they chirped, that the two were reconciled so prettily; how charming their lifelong friendship had been rekindled; how very satisfying for them to reminisce together about their husbands and families. If there was a word of disapproval or censure,

Rosalind knew it would not be expressed today, when all of Bath talked of the happy reunion.

Rosalind walked across the room to greet Fanny. "The meeting at your house began a very admirable reunion. I thank you very much, as I am sure Captain Chadwell and the ladies do too."

"Come," Fanny said. "Stroll with me."

They linked arms and walked toward the orchestra.

"I have heard several accounts of their quite remarkable entry into the Assembly Rooms." Fanny nodded to acquaintances as they passed.

"Indeed it was a triumph. No one can mistake their renewed affection for one another."

"And you followed along, on the arm of Captain Chadwell?"

Rosalind felt her cheeks begin to flush. "Yes. He escorted me in."

"And later you danced?"

"Why, yes. With several men."

"But, it was noted to me, with Captain Chadwell also. How well do you know him, Rosalind?"

"He pushed me into the mud when I was eight years of age. Why?" Rosalind felt a twinge of fear in the pit of her stomach.

"Why just the two ladies I hoped to see this morning," Captain Chadwell said as they approached.

Rosalind tried to keep her face from showing the excitement she felt at seeing him. Fanny would be watching like a hawk. But it was very difficult to keep her eyes off him. He was so handsome and strong-looking, his blue coat so finely cut, his tan waistcoat so elegant, his cravat tied in a simple knot.

Fanny reached out to shake his hand. "Captain, I

congratulate you on the success of your restoration of the ladies' friendship. As I have told Rosalind, no one speaks of anything else this morning."

"We are indebted to you, Miss Gilmore, for providing the setting and the elements of the drama."

"My role was minimal. Any neutral place would have sufficed, but I am proud of my little part in bringing them together."

What was she doing, Rosalind mused, thinking of him as a potential husband? He had never given any indication he wanted to court her or seek her favor. They were friends; that was all. Then why did she feel so empty? What had she expected?

Rosalind felt nervous now in his presence, feeling as though all eyes were on them. She tried to twist her lips into a little smile, with limited success. She and the captain had no reason ever to meet again.

Her throat felt thick with incipient weeping. There had to be a way. And then she remembered her dollhouse, and she gulped back her tears.

"Would you bring Lady Charlotte over to see my dollhouse some afternoon, Captain Chadwell? I think she would enjoy seeing it." She held her breath until he nodded.

"Would Thursday afternoon at two be convenient?"

"Yes. Perhaps Lady Isiline will come to join Lady Rotherford for tea."

He bowed, assenting.

She looked for some sign that he was eager for the meeting, but his face remained impassive.

Now was the moment she wished she knew of a sacred well, one like the Romans believed in, one in which she could drop some coins to ensure the

help of the gods. For it seemed that divine inter-
vention would be needed to win Captain Chadwell's heart.

Eleven

Rosalind turned the small piece of soap round and round in her fingers. How could she turn this little shard into a dog or a cat? She sat near her dollhouse at a table covered with a plain cloth and a selection of knives from the kitchen and a large cake of soap, from which she hacked a slice no bigger than her thumb. Now her project was to make it into the shape of a little dog for the dollhouse.

She had not attempted to carve anything since she was a child when one of the estate workers taught her how to make faces on chestnuts. He did all sorts of wonderful things with a carving knife, like making little baskets out of acorns. Rosalind fervently wished she had paid more attention to his techniques.

With the knife she carefully shaved a thin slice off one edge. The dollhouse was really an excuse to see Captain Chadwell again when he brought Lady Charlotte. If Rosalind could help the lonesome child, the captain would be pleased. She scraped off more soap, narrowing the piece at the top.

Once she had watched a skilled carver at a village fair who whittled whistles, chains, and forest goblins out of wood. He started with a solid piece and shaved off little shreds until he got the form he wanted. Certainly she could do this with the much softer soap. Sugar would also work, but if she was successful enough to show her work to Charlotte, why risk having it eaten in one bite?

She rounded the corners of her bit of soap, trying to find a dog within the soap. Had she not read Michelangelo always knew the figure inside the marble he carved? She giggled out loud. Michelangelo? What a sacrilege!

She chipped away and smoothed the edges until she had the head partially done. But she forgot the ears. Never mind. She kept working, shaving away little curls of soap to form the dog's back and shoulders.

She needed to define a line between the front legs, but she pressed too hard and the whole piece of soap shattered into bits.

She looked down at the mess of soap particles all over the cloth, sighed and brushed them into a pile. She would have to start all over again.

Almost an hour went by before she had a shape that looked a little bit like a dog. If you didn't look too carefully. When Charlotte came to see the house, Rosalind wanted the family to have pets. It was a little test of Captain Chadwell's theory that Charlotte was not afraid of animals but merely used the whim to gain attention.

Rosalind jumped when Evers entered the room. "Lady Rotherford sent me up to see if you need anything, Miss Elliott."

Rosalind saw the shocked expression on the footman's face as he contemplated the scattering of soap fragments in front of her.

She shrugged. "As you see, Evers, I am attempting to carve a little dog from soap. I want it to go in my dollhouse. But I am afraid it is a harder job than I anticipated when I started."

"Yes, carving takes great skill."

"Which I do not have. What to you think of this?" She held up her best attempt a forming a dog.

"I could not say what kind, but it appears to be a canine."

"I am pleased you recognize it. Next, I am going to try a kitten. And tell Grandmother I am in need only of some skill." ·

Philip walked ahead of the sedan chairs carrying Lady Isiline and Charlotte. The past two days he had felt restless, without purpose, though there was still the matter of Charlotte's school to settle. Several times he had started out to call on Miss Elliott, but thought better of it once he neared the Royal Crescent. The two days since he had seen her at the Pump Room had crawled by, unembellished by a single activity that absorbed his attention for more than a few moments. Forty-eight hours of utter monotony, other than his all-too-active mind's eye in which he spent almost every minute in the company of a certain young lady.

Now, he was almost upon her doorstep, his heart hammering as he assisted his great-aunt and Charlotte out of the chairs and into the foyer.

Rosalind stood at the top of the stairs and he swore he had never seen a lovelier sight. Her face was smiling and eager, her lips parted, cheeks luminously pink. Her dress was a shade of blue-green that rivaled the Caribbean Sea on a day without wind, a shade so unique he marveled at how the dyers had matched it. He would have stood gazing at her forever if Charlotte had not tugged at his sleeve.

"Where is the dollhouse?"

Lady Isiline answered quickly. "Mind your manners, Lady Charlotte. We must go upstairs and greet our friends before we view the house."

Philip shook off his desire simply to stare at Miss Elliott and took Charlotte's hand.

A few minutes later, all the courtesies out of the way, they sat in the Rose Salon. Philip looked around and tried to visualize Rosalind spending many hours here. The scene was not what he had envisioned, so assertively pink, so boldly feminine. But of course, it was her grandmother's house and her grandmother's taste. He glanced at Rosalind, who must have been watching him survey the room. She wore a droll expression, as though she were reading his mind. He grinned and gave a little shrug, rewarded by her smile and nod.

Lady Isiline had promised Charlotte the spaniels would be kept below stairs. He thought he might have heard their distant barking upon arrival, but luckily, Charlotte had not. Philip knew she was trying to sit quietly, but before the tea tray arrived, she began to fidget. Captain Chadwell raised his eyebrows. Again Rosalind nodded.

Lady Rotherford and Lady Isiline were deep in conversation already, keen to dissect the latest news of the royal wedding.

Without interrupting their chatter, Philip and Rosalind took Charlotte's hand and led her up two more flights of stairs.

Philip was amazed at the size of the dollhouse standing on a table in the center of the room. Other than its massive presence, the room was sparsely furnished in quiet colors, nothing like the brightness below.

Rosalind put her hand on Charlotte's shoulder and told her about how she played with the house many years ago when she was a child alone.

He strolled over to the other side of the room to get a better view of Rosalind and Charlotte. The little girl's eyes were wide, her look enthralled.

"Here are Mama and Papa." Rosalind handed Charlotte the two little dolls to hold. "And here is the brother and the sister and the baby."

Charlotte peered into the house and reached for a chair.

"Do not touch, Charlotte," Philip cautioned.

Rosalind looked up at him. "Oh, it is all right for Charlotte to play with the dolls. And you can rearrange the furniture and set the dolls wherever you want." She smiled at Philip. "It is all for playing. Anything can be moved and put in another room. That is the fun of dollhouses."

Charlotte took the mama doll from Rosalind and set it in the dining room. "Now she can have dinner."

"Charlotte, I always liked to read a book and have the dolls act out the story. I have a story here, if you would like to hear it."

"Yes, please."

"This story is about the pets the children play with. And here is the dog and the cat."

Charlotte set the soap cat near the little girl. "But the baby does not have a pet. She needs a kitten."

"Yes, perhaps when she grows up a little. Pets are reserved only for older children." Rosalind looked over at Philip. "I am afraid the dog and cat were my favorites and I must have broken them long ago. When they packed up the house to send it here, I think they left out the broken animals. So I have tried to make new ones, but they are only soap."

He was amazed. "How clever of you. I never would have thought of soap."

"I wish I could find some made of wood or china. Perhaps someday, Charlotte, you and I can look in the toy shops."

"I would like that. May I go?" she asked Philip. "Please?"

"Please."

Philip smiled at Charlotte's enthusiasm.

"You need a dog or cat for the dollhouse?" Philip took up the tiny cat. "This is very small. I am not sure my big fingers would be able to make something so little."

"Do you have a pet at your home, Charlotte?" Rosalind asked.

"No, I am frightened of dogs."

"How about kittens?"

"Mama says they have claws that scratch you, and they get fur all over the furniture."

"Yes, they have claws, but most house cats do not use them on people unless they are being hurt." Rosalind opened the book and began to read. *Polly and the Naughty Kitten*.

Philip sat back in his chair and watched as Rosalind read and Charlotte marched the little dolls around the house. He could have watched the scene forever. Rosalind was sweet to his half sister. There was no whining, no complaints, for she was the entire center of attention. Rosalind even encouraged Charlotte to dress the dolls for bedtime. When they were all in their beds, Rosalind marked her place and closed the book.

"I think we should let them sleep now, Charlotte.

Perhaps you can come again tomorrow and we will read the end of the story."

"Does the little girl find her kitty?"

"We will not know until we read the next chapter."

Philip was sorry to call an end to the visit. The hour they had spent with the dollhouse had flown by. He had not been alone with Rosalind for an instant, but he had enjoyed watching and listening. By the time he walked home, after helping his great aunt and sister on their way, Philip was looking forward to the next day with an anticipation that had nothing to do with dollhouses or pink salons.

Lady Rotherford welcomed Pip and Popsy back into the Rose Salon as if they had been banished for months instead of just over an hour. "I could hear my poor darlings barking downstairs, just as sad as they could be."

The spaniels leaped onto her lap, writhing in delight, tails waving in triumph.

"Down there with the awful spiders, you poor dears."

Rosalind chuckled to herself and slipped out of the room, leaving the dogs smothering Lady Rotherford with their sloppy kisses. She had an idea about introducing Charlotte to a certain gray kitten.

The next day, when Captain Chadwell, Lady Isiline, and Lady Charlotte arrived, Rosalind had a box containing Caesar, borrowed from Fanny, in the corner of the dollhouse room. All morning she had been teasing the kitten with a ball of yarn, wearing him almost to exhaustion in the hope that he would be unusually docile when Charlotte and the captain accompanied her upstairs.

"Do not fail me, little one," she whispered to the kitten's already closed eyes as she set him in the box and went to greet Charlotte. How delighted the captain would be if her plan worked.

When they came upstairs to the dollhouse, Rosalind quietly lifted Caesar from his box and settled the kitten in her lap before she opened the book.

Lady Charlotte drew back from the little cat with a sharp intake of breath.

"Do not mind little Caesar here," Rosalind said. "He wants to hear about the kitty in the story too."

Philip stood near Charlotte, as though ready to grab the child if the cat sprang, but Caesar wiggled into a fuzzy ball and stayed in Rosalind's lap.

Rosalind knew Charlotte eyed the kitten fearfully, but she feigned indifference to the child's look. "Better get the family dressed for the next day."

Cautiously, with frequent glances at the kitten, Charlotte put the dress on the little girl. "What is that funny noise?"

"The kitten is purring. When he is content, he makes that little rumbling noise."

"Oh." Charlotte dressed the father and mother, then the little boy. She looked again at the kitten. "Why does he do that?"

"He is telling us he is happy."

"Oh."

Rosalind read on in the story and soon Charlotte seemed oblivious of the kitten. Eventually Philip seated himself and looked less apprehensive.

When she came to the end of the story, the naughty cat restored to Polly, Rosalind offered the book to Charlotte.

Slowly the child edged toward Rosalind's chair

and the sleeping kitten. "Can I touch his fur?" she whispered.

"Why yes, just here on his back. Smooth your hand down like this."

Charlotte reached out a little hand and let her fingers barely touch the cat. Gradually she let her hand cover more of the kitten's back. "He is very soft. Like Mama's fur muff."

Rosalind shifted her leg and Caesar raised his head and blinked at Charlotte.

"His eyes are yellow and black." Her voice was full of wonder.

The kitten tucked his nose under a paw and went back to sleep, purring gently.

Rosalind looked over at Captain Chadwell, who was shaking his head in wonder. "Charlotte, you are being very brave."

"I know," the child answered.

Rosalind heard the tapping of her grandmother's cane. "Your great-aunt and Lady Rotherford are coming up. Just think how proud they will be to see you pet the kitten."

Lady Isiline was the first through the door. "I could not let those stairs keep me from seeing this wondrous house. Charlotte has talked of nothing else since yesterday."

The elderly woman, followed by Lady Rotherford, came round to look at the house, but also noticed the kitten, who had again raised his head at the new voice.

"What have we here?" Lady Isiline peered down at the kitten which returned her stare.

"Rosalind, where did that animal come from?" Lady Rotherford's voice was stern.

Before Rosalind could answer, Popsy and Pip burst

into the room, barking uproariously. Caesar leapt to
his feet, hissing, his fur standing out to double his
size. In an instant he was on the floor running from
the dogs, right up the curtains to the velvet pelmet
near the ceiling, where he spit furiously at the dogs
jumping up and down below.

Charlotte shrieked and huddled in Philip's lap,
Lady Rotherford sputtered incoherently and Lady
Isiline's mouth hung open in dismay. Rosalind
looked from one to another. How could she ever
explain this disaster?

Then she looked again at Charlotte, who actually
seemed to be laughing. "He climbed right up to the
top. Did you see that?" She actually clapped her
hands in glee.

Rosalind rushed over to grab the two dogs in her
arms. "Where did you come from?"

Jaspers and Evers, both red-faced and panting,
stood in the doorway. "Beg pardon, milady. The fellows burst by Cook."

"Poor little darlings. Better take them back downstairs."

"Yes, milady." The butler and the footman each
took a squirming spaniel from Rosalind and started
back down the stairs.

"And please send someone up with a ladder,"
Rosalind said.

"Did you see that, Aunt Izzy?" Charlotte was still
full of wonder at the kitten's flight.

"Yes, Charlotte. But now what is he going to do?"
Lady Isiline frowned up at the kitten, which had
ceased hissing and now cried piteously.

"I think he is very frightened to be up so high,"
Rosalind said.

Charlotte began to cry. "Poor Caesar. Please, do not fall. Hold on. Oh, save him, Philip."

"Even if I stand on a chair, I can not reach him."

Charlotte buried her face in Rosalind's skirts, sobbing.

Rosalind smoothed the child's hair. "There now, Charlotte. They will be along with a ladder any moment."

Philip paced back a forth below the mewling kitten. "Perhaps I should go give the men a hand."

"No," Charlotte moaned. "If he falls, you must catch him, Philip." She raised her tear-stained face. "Please do not leave."

To Rosalind it seemed ages before Evers and the kitchen boy managed to put the ladder into place. Just as the boy reached a rung high enough to grasp the kitten, Caesar gave a piteous cry and scampered down the drapery as rapidly as he had climbed up.

"Ooooh," Charlotte yelped.

Captain Chadwell dove for the door and shut it just in time to prevent Caesar from racing through it. He grabbed the kitten and held him close and tight. "Now there, my fiery one, just calm your little self." The kitten struggled for a moment, then seemed to realize he was in a place of safety and lay still.

The boy backed down the ladder and helped Evers, still flushed with the exertion, carry the ladder out of the room.

Captain Chadwell set the kitten in his box. "I think the commotion is over. Caesar will soon be fast asleep again."

Lady Rotherford bristled. "Rosalind, the idea of having a feline up here. I am appalled."

"I will return him to Fanny later, Grandmother. I am afraid my scheme did not work out very well."

Rosalind's step was dispirited, her feelings downhearted as she carried the box containing Caesar to Fanny Gilmore's house. Her plan had been a complete failure. Instead of gracefully introducing Charlotte to the kitten, the afternoon turned into a catastrophe. Instead of helping Captain Chadwell ease the little girl's eccentricities, she probably worsened them. He would not be pleased with the consequences.

At Fanny's, she confessed every detail of the entire fiasco.

Fanny cuddled the kitten. "He seems to have survived the experience without harm."

"I hope so." Rosalind propped her elbow on the arm of her chair and rested her chin on her hand. "Grandmother is quite displeased with me and I am sure Captain Chadwell and Lady Isiline wish I had not meddled with Lady Charlotte's sensibilities."

"As for Captain Chadwell, you may be better off seeing no more of him."

"What?" Rosalind straightened up in a trice. "What do you mean?"

Fanny sighed. "You know I do not indulge in idle gossip. Nor do I encourage people to tell me tales of any kind. But I could not avoid remarks by several people who are concerned for your welfare, my friend."

"I do not understand."

"Rosalind, there are people who say Captain Chadwell has a poor reputation, earned long ago, probably when he was young and foolish. Those old stories are not my concern."

"I am surprised you listen to such ancient tittle-tattle."

Fanny stroked the sleeping kitten. "When he ran off with another man's wife, he was hardly more than a lad. As far as I can tell, no one has any more stories about lightskirts or opera dancers, much less other men's wives. Since his one all-too-public affair, apparently he has led an exemplary life."

"Exactly!" Rosalind wore an exultant smile. "Then there is no reason I should avoid his company."

"His old exploits are not the problem. Actually, I would not say a word against him, except that I know how you feel about fortune hunters."

"Fortune hunters? Oh, come now, Fanny. Not Chadwell, certainly."

"I was told that he is here in Bath with Lady Isiline because he hankers after her funds. His eldest brother will inherit his father's estate and nothing will come to him, so he is trying, it is said, to ingratiate himself with his great-aunt and be named in her will."

"I can not believe it." Rosalind felt cold all over, and the chill made her tremble.

"I would not tell you to hurt you or break your heart. But you must find out if it is true. We must investigate."

"I do not know what to think or how to proceed."

"And you have fallen in love with him?" Fanny asked.

"Yes. No. The time we have spent together was directed toward our little project to rekindle friendship between Grandmother and Lady Isiline.

Fanny shrugged. "I hope you have not lost your heart."

Rosalind kept the state of her heart to herself. "I do not understand why people are saying such things about a man who served the Crown all through the war."

"One thing about Bath gossip. Sooner or later everything and everyone has their turn for scrutiny, all other merits aside. Just as an old scandal involving the captain has been uncovered, so has his wealth or lack of it. How many men are in Bath more than a week before the size of their pocketbooks are well known?"

"But known with what accuracy? Who is to say that the information so randomly passed about here is true or false? Fanny, you of all people to pass along such things. I never would have believed it of you."

"Rosalind, I am only trying to do what is best for you. I do not want you to be hurt. In the past, you have complained about the way most men seem more interested in your inheritance than your character or concerns. You said they care more for your bank account than anything else."

Rosalind stared down at the floor, saying nothing.

Fanny continued. "Believe me, Ros, I am only trying to help you. I myself find Captain Chadwell handsome and charming. If I were ten years younger, he might turn my head. You need to learn if he is truly on the lookout for a wealthy match."

Rosalind's voice wavered as she spoke. "He has never spoken a word about his plans for the future. He says he is only here to put Charlotte in school and to see Lady Isiline comfortably established. I believe he plans to move on once he has accomplished his purposes."

"Please, Rosalind, do not be angry with me. Just take this information and use it to your advantage. If you truly care for him, you are capable of making your own decisions."

Rosalind gathered up her shawl and reticule. "I am not angry with you, Fanny. I am surprised and disappointed to hear what is being said. I shall have to go home and think."

"I am so sorry to be the bearer of bad news, my dear," Fanny said as they went to the door. "I hope you will forgive me."

"There is nothing to forgive." Rosalind gave Fanny a distracted hug before she left.

Twelve

Rosalind sat in the garden and stared at a grassy patch. She did not look at the abundant roses flowing over the trellis nor did she notice their sweet perfume. She felt utterly crushed. All her plans and dreams were trampled to ruins.

Philip Chadwell, a fortune hunter? How could it be?

He was so handsome and strong, his blue coat so finely cut, his tan waistcoat so elegant. The very thought of him as a fortune hunter made her laugh. Why, it was ridiculous. A man with no funds does not have a wardrobe from London's finest tailors. And yet he never said he had more than his compensation from the navy.

Just imagine a tiny part of what Fanny said was true, Rosalind told herself. But he had not come to Bath to wheedle money out of his great-aunt. He was here to help. Or so he said. The libertine charge was ancient history, too long ago to matter. Anyway, she had often heard it said that the best husbands were the reformed rakes.

Wait! What was she doing, thinking of him as a potential husband? Had he ever given any indication he wanted to court her or seek her favor? They were friends; that was all. Then why did she feel so betrayed? What had she expected? Why would he have been any different from any other man she knew?

Fanny was the only woman of her acquaintance who had the brains to stay unmarried by choice. She said men came in a limited number of varieties. There were men who were out and out looking for an heiress; at least one could admire them for their honesty. There were men who pretended to have no interest in dowries or settlements but secretly counted on having her money in their pockets before the wedding breakfast was concluded. And there might be men who had so much money of their own they did not have the slightest interest in a lady's income or her property.

If such a man ever arrived in Bath, Rosalind would have been more than surprised. She would have been over the moon!

If it had not been for Miss Elliott's snub this morning in the Pump Room, Philip would have been exultant. His visit to the Standard Academy for Young Ladies of Quality had been a complete success. The headmistress was cooperative and accommodating. They were quite used to dealing with children in need of guidance without trying to break their spirit. And they were willing to accept Charlotte in a fortnight.

He felt as if a great burden had been lifted from his back. Yet his satisfaction was tinged with frustration. He ought to be eager to set his departure from Bath. But he could not think of any reason why Miss Elliott had been so out of sorts with him this morning. If he had done something to offend her, he wished to make amends. But he couldn't think of anything.

He had intended to tell her how Charlotte suddenly was begging for a kitten. He had hoped to spend a little time gloating over their success reuniting the two old ladies. But she hadn't given him so much as a direct look.

Neither had she appeared at her best. Perhaps she had not slept well. Still the questions nagged at him. Was he oversensitive this morning or had she been as cold as ice? Almost impolite, as uncharacteristic of her as that sounded.

He strode up and down a few of Bath's steepest hills, oblivious of the gigs and sedan chairs, carts and drays, the noise of horses and bustle of shoppers. He avoided the fashionable areas of town. Eventually, when he found no answers to his perplexing uncertainties, he headed back to the house he had leased for Lady Isiline, Charlotte, and himself. Later perhaps he would call on Miss Elliott with the excuse of asking where he might find another Caesar.

When he turned the corner onto New King Street, he stopped so suddenly he almost lost his balance. Three large vehicles filled the pavement before his house. A mélange of trunks and scurrying footmen surrounded the coaches. He moved closer and his heart dropped to his ankles. One of the equipages bore his father's crest, and the footmen all appeared to be in the Sedgewyck livery.

It appeared the Earl of Sedgewyck and his wife had arrived in Bath. He almost turned and fled, but thought better of it. No matter what the consequences, he needed to defend the rights of Lady Isiline; Henrietta would banish his elderly great-aunt, bad joints and all, to the attics if she got half a chance.

Rosalind declined to accompany her grand-mother to a luncheon party at Lady Brandle's, excusing herself to make preparations for her approaching departure for Delphine's wedding. Not that she was looking forward to the journey.

Of course she wanted to share in her friend's happiness. And of course she was curious to meet the paragon of masculine virtues Delphine described in her letters, the man of her dreams.

Man of her dreams. Rosalind sat on her bed and thought about the man of her own dreams. Captain Chadwell a fortune hunter? It could not be. Fanny's informant must have been mistaken. He might not be a man of great wealth, but to think of him toadying up to Lady Isiline simply to qualify for her bequests, why the thought was repellent indeed.

She opened her armoire and confronted the array of gowns inside. There was to be a ball on the eve of the wedding, Delphine had written. Rosalind wondered if she would need a new gown. Bath was full of modistes but how current they were with London fashions she did not know.

Oh, what does it matter? She could wear any old thing. She slammed the door shut. The only person whose good opinions she might seek had turned out to be a man of straw instead of a hero of iron. The dreams she had of Captain Chadwell were dwindling to dust.

But she would not let herself dissolve into a puddle of tears. Poor Cinnamon would be spending too much time in her stall while Rosalind was away.

Why not take the mare out for a good, long run every day until she left?

She changed quickly and told Evers of her plan on the way out. In just half an hour she was mounted and heading for the hills above Bath, a groom following along this time. If, by chance, she met Captain Chadwell this afternoon, she would not succumb to any of his wretched kisses. That much was certain.

Urging the mare to a canter, she hissed his name aloud. "Philip Chadwell, cad, trickster, swindler, charlatan, liar." When she exhausted her vocabulary, she repeated the list. An empty pleasure, she thought, but useful nonetheless.

Rosalind assisted her grandmother out of the chair and into the Pump Room. Lady Isiline was already there, and sat with strangers, a man of about sixty years and a younger woman dressed in the fussiest height of fashion.

"Who is that with Isiline," Lady Rotherford whispered.

"I have no idea. Do you wish to go to her?"

"Yes."

As they made their way slowly to Lady Isiline's group, Rosalind watched the younger woman, who talked without stopping, and noted Lady Isiline's disapproving expression.

"Good morning, Isiline," Lady Rotherford said as they approached.

"Anne, good morning. May I make known to you my nephew Lord Sedgewyck and his wife?"

Oh my. This was the woman Captain Chadwell held in a minimum of regard.

"George, you remember Lady Rotherford and her granddaughter, Miss Elliott. Henrietta, Lady Rotherford is my oldest friend."

Lord Sedgewyck rose with a grimace of pain and bowed to them. Henrietta, cut off in midsentence, nodded, a sour look on her face.

Henrietta assumed control of the conversation. "I insisted my husband come take the cure. His pain has made my life a misery. He complains from dawn to dusk."

"As if you ever see the dawn," Lord Sedgewyck muttered, nearly under his breath.

Henrietta paid him no heed. "We must find a house immediately. Aunt Isiline's chambers are quite insufficient for all of us."

Rosalind glanced at Lady Isiline, whose agonized expression clearly indicated her agreement on the point.

Lady Sedgewyck jabbered on without a breath. "I require the very finest accommodations. Have you a recommendation, Lady Rotherford?"

Rosalind tried to gain her grandmother's attention and shake her head, but Lady Rotherford was looking intently at Lady Sedgewyck with a sort of stricken expression.

"I know of nothing at the moment . . ." Lady Rotherford spoke very slowly.

Henrietta grimaced. "You mean all the houses in the Royal Crescent are let? I should be very disappointed if that were so. I understand that is where you reside. Are none of your neighbors in London or abroad? So many people have gone to France now that the war is over and I am so hoping to see Paris myself, but with my husband's afflictions, it seems to be impossible at the moment."

Rosalind sincerely hoped that none of the thirty Royal Crescent residences was available for lease, though she knew of several, perhaps half a dozen, where the usual occupants were gone. The thought of having the loquacious Henrietta, Lady Sedgewyck, on their doorstep whenever she wished to step outside was daunting indeed. And it would be worse for her grandmother while Rosalind was away. The poor lady would have no peace at all.

While Henrietta rattled on, Rosalind looked more carefully at her. Despite the warm weather, she carried a fur muff and wore a dark tippet around her shoulders. The fur was thick and glossy, obviously expensive. No doubt its quality was the reason she wore it, to demonstrate her prominence to everyone in Bath. The effect of that ploy was likely to be exactly the reverse. The high sticklers here in the Pump Room were connoisseurs of societal pretensions. Lady Sedgewyck might indeed be a countess, but her tastes would hitherto be suspect as ostentatious.

The thought caused Rosalind a brief pang of glee, quickly squelched by reality. She resented the arrival of the Sedgewycks just when her grandmother and Lady Isiline were beginning their new friendship. There were bound to be snags to their intimacy now.

"As for Philip," Lady Sedgewyck rattled on, "the earl says he must marry money. Absolutely essential for his future, he says . . ."

Rosalind felt her hopes sink into the depths of despair. Philip's lack of money must be a fact if his father was worried. She tried to keep her face from reflecting her glum feelings as her heart yearned to break into sobs.

After one of the longest half hours she had ever
endured, Rosalind feared their sojourn at the Pump
Room would last forever. Henrietta—for Rosalind
could hardly think of her as anything more than a
gabbler, hardly a lady—never slowed in her long-
winded recital of tribulations she endured, triumphs
she achieved, important connections she enjoyed,
and compliments she garnered. Not only was her
presentation one-sided and self-centered, it allowed
for no commentary from her listeners, who pretended to be engrossed and captivated by the lady's
consequence.

Just when Rosalind was about to excuse herself
and flee, Henrietta announced she had many purchases to make. She intended to inspect the shops
of Milsom Street. Rosalind found herself pitying
the poor merchants. There were looks of relief on
her grandmother's and Lady Isiline's faces. Lord
Sedgewyck, who had long ago nodded off, struggled awake.

Henrietta issued a flurry of orders to her husband and Lady Isiline before she finally made her
exit, sweeping out of the room with the pompous
gestures of a bogus queen exiting her throne room.

When Lady Sedgewyck left, a stilted silence fell
over the group. Rosalind was certain that both Lady
Isiline and her grandmother were bursting to com-
ment on the departed lady and her manners, but
obviously with the earl on hand, nothing could be
said. Rosalind herself was overcome with pity for
the earl. And poor Charlotte, to have such a
mother. No wonder the child was a handful, with
such a pattern to follow.

And what of Philip? How would he take his father's arrival in the house he had leased for his

great-aunt and his half sister? Rosalind knew, without seeing a specific example, Henrietta's demeanor must be an affront to Captain Chadwell too.

After a few moments, when everyone busied themselves with another sip of the water or, in Rosalind's case, searched in her reticule for nothing at all to cover the awkward moment, Lord Sedgewyck used his cane to push himself to his feet.

"I see Mr. Tuttle just came in and I shall join him for a moment, ladies, if you will excuse me."

The ladies expressed approval, and he slowly limped away. When she had watched him sit down with Mr. Tuttle, Lady Isiline heaved a great sigh.

"I truly feel for Sedgewyck. He never has a moment's peace. Whatever affection caused him to marry that woman has been long ago extinguished, in my opinion. Is it any wonder he feigns almost total deafness?"

Lady Rotherford nodded so vigorously her bonnet came untied. "How are you managing in New King Street?"

"She almost moved me out of my bedchamber until Philip arrived at the house and set things straight. He had a bed moved into the library, ostensibly so his father would not have to climb two flights."

"Admirable," Lady Rotherford murmured.

"But now Philip has no hideaway of his own except a temporary bedchamber under the eaves. He will be gone from Bath tomorrow morning."

Rosalind tried not to let her ambivalent feelings show on her face, forcing a little smile. "Oh, is he heading back to London?"

"I would not blame him if he headed for the Antipodes. Henrietta alternates between treating him

like a servant and flirting with him like a Covent
Garden nun."

"Isiline!" Lady Rotherford's exclamation of
shock was instantly betrayed by a snort of giggling.

Lady Isiline grinned too. "Pardon me, my dear.
Rosalind, you did not hear me say that. But I cannot approve of her conduct, which she inherits
from a father whose dissolute behavior was a continuing scandal since we first heard of him thirty
years ago. Do you not recall, Anne? He had not
taken up his barony yet and as Mr. Terrance he was
quite the rogue. Terrance the Terrible he was
called. And when he married the mousy Miss
Carstairs, we all pitied her."

Lady Rotherford's distaste showed in her scowl.
"I had forgotten."

Rosalind let the conversation carry on without her.
Philip was leaving Bath. The thought resounded in
her head as if announced by the continual crash of
cymbals, throbbing painfully in her ears. Even if he
was a fortune hunter, as appeared to be the case, she
would miss him.

Where would he go and how would she ever find
him again? Lady Isiline would hear from him, it was
certain. Rosalind would have to ask and the old
ladies might get the wrong idea. So far they seem
oblivious of the attraction between them. At least
she did not have to face the mortification of more
Bath gossip about herself and fortune hunters. Yet
it seemed an empty victory indeed.

Thirteen

Rosalind's head ached by the time she arrived at Greyneck Abbey, home of Delphine's family. Nell and Evers, who had won the competition downstairs to have a trip away from Bath, had enjoyed their last evening at the Red Lion Inn and they were looking forward to meeting a new group of people and renewing their acquaintance with the servants who had come to Bath the last time Delphine had visited.

They were in good spirits the entire way, while Rosalind had lost herself in alternative bouts of dreamy thoughts centering on a certain former naval captain, or on complications for her grandmother and Lady Isiline. All of Bath would find Henrietta quite the object of attention now, and not more than a few days would pass before someone had ascertained every detail of her parentage and upbringing. Rosalind had little sympathy for the earl. After all, he had gotten himself into the situation by seeking a second wife. He had long ago had many children, his heir and two spares, his two daughters, his lineage well-protected. He should have found himself a comfortable widow near his own age with whom to spend the rest of his life instead of taking on a young, grasping, and avaricious female who had probably bewitched him. If Rosalind had ever considered marriage with a much older man, one hour spent in the company of the Sedgewycks had certainly cured her of any temptation.

Thoughts like these had clogged her poor brain all through the long hours in the carriage. Despite its supposedly well-sprung construction and the softness of the cushions within, she found the journey tedious and numbing. She spent hours wondering where Captain Chadwell was going, with whom he would visit, and if she would ever see him again. She tried to convince herself he had not taken a corner of her heart with him. She spent more hours trying to concoct a way to excuse herself for the rudeness she had shown him that morning in the Pump Room. Once she had heard what Fanny reported, she had been incapable of speaking to him. She greatly feared a single word might lead to a flood of tears.

She knew he had been surprised and distressed by her coldness. At that very moment she had been more confused than anything. She had hardly slept a wink because of the disturbing thoughts that raged through her mind.

Some of her thoughts had traveled in forbidden directions, far from propriety and into the realm of fantasy. If she, like the characters in a novel she had read, were imprisoned in a dark castle, Philip Chadwell would find her and rescue her from the evil clutches of some despicable mad nobleman. Once she was rescued, Philip would carry her to a chamber with a huge canopied bed layered with silken sheets and strewn with velvet pillows. And he would cover her with kisses and turn her body to molten fire. Those thoughts brought her warm sensations of languor that lasted just long enough to hit the next rough spot in the road. Jostled back into reality, she thought again of how rude she had been to him, of how she might never see him again. She did not care if he had five pence to his name. She did not care what anyone said about him or about her. Let them talk.

But he was gone.

And why did she think he cared for her anyway? Yes, they were friends and had shared a successful mission. He had kissed her once and begged her pardon in the next breath. What kind of eternal passion did that demonstrate? Her dreams seemed foolish in that light.

When they finally arrived at Greyneck Abbey, the Epleys' estate, Rosalind was glad she was able to go directly to her room and rest before seeing Delphine. She needed to sort herself out and concentrate on her friend's happiness. She did not want to be a sourpuss when she met Delphine's dream man.

Fortunately she was able to nap for an hour before Delphine burst into her room.

"Rosie, I am sorry I was not here to greet you. Perry and I were seeing that his parents are comfortably settled in the Dower House. Oh, I am sorry I woke you."

Rosalind sat up and shook her head. "I am fine. I did not mean to fall asleep."

"Your journey must have been exhausting. But I am so glad you came and I want you to meet Perry. Oh, Rosie, he is so wonderful."

Rosalind stood and stretched. "Then I must do my hair and put on a less rumpled gown. It would not do for you to have an old friend who looks untidy and worn to shreds."

"You? You have always been the loveliest of ladies and a few stray curls will not dim your looks, my dear. Come, give me a hug."

Rosalind squeezed her friend. "Del, I am so happy for you. You have found your dearest love."

Delphine spun away and spread her arms wide, twirling around in delight. "I never would have believed I could be so happy."

Rosalind felt her heart swelling with happiness for her friend. All her qualms and quandaries were pushed aside in her joy.

"Then I shall ring for Nell and put myself to rights."

"Come down to the morning room as soon as you are ready. Perry and I will wait for you there."

Hardly a quarter of an hour had passed when Rosalind peeked into the morning room.

Peregrine Sanborne stood beside Delphine at the window, holding her hand and looking over the spring garden beyond.

"Rosalind, may I introduce my betrothed, Mr. Peregrine Sanborne," Delphine said.

"I am most pleased to know you. My betrothed's best friend," the gentleman added.

"And I am indeed happy to know you, Mr. Sanborne. Delphine has written about you, crossing and recrossing her pages with a catalog of your virtues."

He had an angelic smile, Rosalind thought to herself. Rather younger than she had expected, but handsome, a square face, wavy light brown hair, and eyes as blue as Delphine's.

"Tomorrow evening we will have a ball for all our neighbors and friends." Delphine's high color evidenced her pleasure at the coming festivities. "The ceremony is the next morning and the wedding breakfast here afterwards."

Peregrine captured his fiancée's hand again. "Then we shall depart for Dover and by boat to Belgium."

Rosalind listened to a recital of all the wonderful places the couple intended to visit on the Continent. "You will be gone for months."

They gazed into each other's faces. "Yes, but we shall return before Christmas. Perry's family gathers in Derbyshire and I will meet two of his sisters there for the first time. Both of them are—"

"Indisposed," Perry said quickly.

"Increasing," Delphine said at the same moment, her cheeks growing even pinker.

Rosalind almost laughed aloud at their sweet confusion.

Just then another face peered around the edge of the morning room door.

"Perry?" a man's voice said.

"Oliver!" Perry dashed forward and drew the man into the room, to Delphine's side. "My dearest, here is my very best friend, Oliver Thorne. We were together at Eton and at King's College too."

Rosalind watched as the three of them exchanged greetings. Perry's friend Oliver was almost his twin, though dressed a touch more in the mode of a town swell. They wore similar coats of dark blue with large brass buttons. Where Perry's waistcoat was a gold brocade, Oliver's boasted puce-and-white stripes.

Mr. Thorne looked to be a pleasant enough young man, with the same smooth manners and air of ingenuousness. Compared to the rugged brawn of Captain Chadwell, they both appeared insignificant.

Delphine gestured to Rosalind and drew her near. "And Rosalind, Miss Elliott, is my very best friend, Mr. Thorne."

He bowed to Rosalind and gave her a most charming smile. "I am pleased to know you, Miss Elliott. These are indeed happy days for our mutual friends."

Rosalind curtsied. "Indeed yes. I have only just arrived myself, and I could not be happier to see their joy in each other."

Perry recited the plans for the next few days and upon finding that Oliver had left his things at the Dower House, suggested they all four walk together in the gardens and eventually to the Dower House.

The weather was as fine as England ever had to offer. Even the skies smiled on the happy couple with all the felicity they appeared to deserve. By the time dinner was over and the ladies retired to the drawing room, Rosalind had renewed her friendship with Delphine's mother and was pleased to make the acquaintance of Perry's mama, a plump woman with an obvious taste for the gemstones she wore in profusion.

Delphine could not wait to sit down on a satin sofa with Rosalind while the two older ladies admired the collection of oriental ivories arrayed on the side table.

"Tell me what you think." Delphine sounded breathless with enthusiasm. "Is he not wonderful?"

Rosalind made the most of her first opportunity to tell Delphine of the innumerable fine qualities she had discovered in Mr. Peregrine Sanborne. From his superior forehead to his fine hands graced by a handsome signet ring, from his amiable charm to his learned recitation of the botanical names of many of the garden's flowers, he was indeed a paragon.

Delphine giggled. "Perry the paragon. Oh, yes, Rosalind, you have found the perfect description. For a long time I could not believe he was truly interested in me. But now I know that he is really devoted. He has written me such poems, Rosalind. Such beauty. Not even Byron could compose better."

Rosalind hugged Delphine. "I am so very delighted for you."

"And now, it will soon be your turn, Rosalind. I feel it inside." She clasped her hand to her heart. "You too will find a man you love, I just know it. And very soon."

"Oh, I am not so sure." Rosalind felt a lump in her throat. Was Delphine truly so perceptive, or had she mentioned Captain Chadwell in one of her letters? And if Captain Chadwell was the man she could love, had she already lost him?

"And perhaps, just perhaps, that man will turn out to be Mr. Thorne. Would that not be perfect, Rosie? If we are married to best friends, we could live near one another and be close forever."

Rosalind cleared her throat and pushed away the image of Captain Chadwell. "Mr. Thorne and I have exchanged only a few words and almost every one of them concerned you and Perry."

"You must agree he is fine-looking, and very able. Like Perry, he is a second son. That is part of their strong friendship. Both of them have had to make their own way in the world. But rather than go into the church as Perry has, Mr. Thorne has remained a scholar, studying the law, I believe."

Rosalind squeezed Delphine's hand. "I shall be on my best behavior for Mr. Thorne and all of your guests, I assure you. If he takes a liking to me, then we shall see."

"But I am impatient to see you as happy as I am, Rosalind. Never say that staying in Bath with all those elderly ladies has tainted your enjoyment of a little flirtation."

Rosalind laughed, about to reassure Delphine when the gentlemen came into the room, and the moment was lost as her friend immediately dashed into Perry's arms.

The wedding breakfast finally concluded in the late afternoon. Rosalind slipped away from the celebrants as soon as the newly married couple left in a carriage bedecked with garlands of daisies.

The tears Rosalind shed during the service at the little stone church were tears of joy, she told herself. Delphine was as radiant as every bride should be. As Mrs. Sandborne, she gazed with adoring eyes at her husband all through the festivities.

Now that the bridal pair had departed, Rosalind at last felt she could stop smiling and indulge her real feelings. She was ashamed to admit her envy. Unseemly, unladylike, unworthy. Whatever the negative feelings she felt, she hoped she had hidden them well. She had tried to keep a proper smile on her face, cheery words of encouragement on her tongue.

Now all she wanted was to be alone for an hour, to reorder her thoughts and prepare for one more evening of smiling and congratulations. In the morning she could go home to Bath, no longer forcing the grin on her face.

She headed down a path toward the less manicured areas of the garden. A place of grotesque beauty, so adored by the likes of Repton and his ilk. She found a rustic seat beside the pool downstream from the waterfall. Its rushing cascade provided a background more welcome than the merry voices, laughter, clink of glasses, chatter of voices. She stared into the water, where flashes of gold and silver revealed the pattern of darting fish among the narrow shafts of sunlight that pierced the heavy tree cover. Thick tufts of ferns filled spaces between the stones and the water.

"Miss Elliott?"

She was sorry there was no place to hide. She was not in the mood for any more conversation, especially with Oliver Thorne. Too late, she thought as he rounded the giant yew that shaded the pool.

"May I invade your privacy for a moment?" His quiet demeanor hardly deserved the violence of the thoughts she directed toward him.

"I looked for a cool spot, away from all the people."

"No matter how congenial, a mass of people can become overwhelming, I agree."

"Please be seated, if you wish." She moved to the edge of the bench.

He walked over to the pool and looked it over before sitting beside her.

"I do not know how the day could have been improved upon. The heavens blessed the new Mr. and Mrs. Sanborne."

"A truly happy occasion." Rosalind folded her hands in her lap.

"Do you leave tomorrow?"

"Yes, if I can extract my man from his fascination with one of Mrs. Epley's kitchen girls. My maid tells me he is quite besotted."

"Weddings have a way of inspiring people to think of romance." Mr. Thorne looked away from her and stared at the pool. "I must say something of that nature has affected me."

Rosalind flinched. "Oh, I am sure the feeling will pass once you go back to your regular activities."

"Perhaps. But I was thinking I might make a visit to Bath sometime soon."

She forced a smile and gave a little laugh. "I hope you are not suffering from aching joints or the pains of gout."

"Oh, no. My suffering is of a quite different nature."

"I dare not speculate on what that might be, Mr. Thorne."

"No, perhaps I should not be precipitate in my assumptions. I do wish to know, however, if I might call upon you and your grandmother. I find myself quite taken with your descriptions of that lady."

Rosalind could not remember much of what she had said about her life in Bath. "I assure you we live a very quiet life. Excitement and Bath are words hardly ever spoken in the same sentence. But I am sure Lady Rotherford and I would be pleased to welcome you to the city."

"Then I shall see you there before the month is out."

Rosalind wished the fact brought her even a wisp of agreeable feeling.

Later, long after she should have been asleep, Rosalind wondered about Mr. Oliver Thorne. He was certainly acceptable on all accounts, modest in bearing, attractive in looks. He was all that was polite. Not a trace of the libertine or the fortune hunter. There was nothing she could criticize in him. And nothing she could extol either.

If she made a list of qualities she wished for in a man, and she often had done exactly that, he would fulfill every requirement. There was only one way in which he was deficient.

He was not Captain Philip Chadwell.

Fourteen

The dark bay gelding turned out to have been an excellent buy, Philip thought as he moved along at a steady trot. The mount he named Neptune was a sturdy beast with the ground-covering pace and endurance the seller had guaranteed. The occasional use of a rental horse had been sufficient for his stay in Bath, where he walked almost everywhere and rode out only for exercise.

And to meet Miss Elliott. Blast and damn, there was the image of her in his very arms again. How could he have let his brain become so mushy? Any little stray thought that popped up could easily dominate his thinking. Ha! As if thoughts of Rosalind just strayed into his head. Thinking about her more closely resembled a permanent state of mind. He and Neptune had made good time yesterday on their way to Portsmouth. Last night Philip had a splendid evening with some of his old navy friends who were still at the base, an evening spent talking over old times and catching up on which of his compatriots had left the navy and which ones were still commanding vessels. The meeting was just what the doctor ordered, worth gallons of that stinking medicinal water and months of idle chatter at Bath.

Today, he headed to an estate just west of Lymington, south of the New Forest near a village known as Lymore, one of several small properties the agent in Portsmouth told him was available for purchase. Some of his listings had been to the east in Hampshire but Philip did not want to be too close to any of the newly fashionable channel resorts. Any move in Brighton's direction made him rule those out. He had no taste for the crowd of fribbles that centered around the Prince Regent.

At a crossroads, he stopped the horse again and took out the map the agent had drawn of the route to Lymore Park. One thing was sure, he would not have a great many uninvited guests dropping in because they were passing nearby. He turned Neptune's head toward the south and over a small rise came upon a small village. The men sitting in the yard of the Bell and Anchor gave him a look of interest. Strangers probably did not pass this way very often. But he doubted he looked the part of a revenue agent. That is surely for whom they were on the lookout.

He did not stop, though he would return later, after he had inspected the house.

The bell tower of the church was the signpost saying he had arrived. The house was not far beyond the churchyard, set off by a towering hedge badly in need of trimming. The house itself was set on level ground, three stories of gray lichened stone and topped by many clusters of chimneys.

The weedy drive circled around to the back on the side away from the church and he followed it to a group of outbuildings. It seemed there was a walled kitchen garden, stables, probably a laundry and a brewhouse. None of the buildings was in the best of repair but none in imminent danger of collapse either.

He called out as he dismounted and a man came out of the stables.

"Sir?"

"I am looking for Mr. Fanning, owner of Lymore Park."

"Mr. Fanning's not here, but he be lookin' to sell. Miz June kin show ye through, if ye be interested. I'll water the horse. He needin' eats?"

"Just a bit of hay, if you do not mind. Over here?"

"Door on the left be the kitchen."

"Thanks." Philip flipped the man a crown for his trouble.

He rapped briskly on the door, then opened it. "Mrs. June?"

A woman as broad as she was tall appeared in the kitchen door. "Yessir?"

"My name is Philip Chadwell, Captain Chadwell, formerly of His Majesty's Navy. The land agent in Portsmouth said this property is for sale."

"Indeed, that be so, Cap'n." She brushed the flour from her expansive bosom. "I kin take ye round."

She led the way through a pantry and into a dining room. The ceiling was low and beamed. South-facing diamond-paned windows let in the sunshine.

Philip looked around and saw Rosalind at the table with the light making a halo of her curls. She seemed to belong in the room. Aside from the faded curtains the furnishings looked sound.

"Are all the furnishings for sale?"

"Far as I know."

The dining room opened into a large two-storied

hall, obviously from an earlier era. Off the hall were two drawing rooms and a library, done up in the style of the early eighteenth century. The library particularly appealed to Philip for it boasted a large globe, an object he longed to possess. She would stand beside it while he traced his voyages and told her of his experiences on the *Venture.* She had said she wanted to know more about where he had traveled.

How lovely she would look in this drawing room, pouring tea in front of the fire. Perhaps with a little gray cat on her lap.

Upstairs, Mrs. June led the way to the main bedchamber, a large room also facing south and filled with sunshine, when Mrs. June threw wide the curtains. A huge tester bed stood on the long wall. He could see her there, waiting for him to join her, a shy smile on her lovely lips.

The panoply of visions that crowded his brain filled him with pleasure, and he dragged himself back to reality. What was he doing seeing Rosalind in this house? Where did those images come from?

"Thank you, Mrs. June. I appreciate your efforts. Obviously the house is kept in fine order."

"Some rooms be a bit shabby . . . but yer lady'll have ideas 'bout that."

Philip shook his head to clear it. Yes, his lady would have some views on the house. His lady.

Fifteen

Rosalind fingered the new shawl, the softest she ever owned, just one of her many recent purchases. When she returned from Delphine's wedding, Grandmother had almost dragged her into the shops, where Rosalind indulged in a flurry of spending. Rosalind had not thought her spell of being blue-deviled had been quite so obvious. Now she had a tall stack of boxes in the corner of her bedchamber and she found she did not want any of the fripperies inside them.

The main advantage of the shopping excursions had been to hide her gloomy moods more effectively from Grandmother. She put the shawl back into its box. Rather than wear it herself, she could give it to Fanny.

Nell scratched on the door. "Miss Elliott, Lady Rotherford has a guest and asks that you come to the Rose Salon."

Rosalind's heart leaped into her throat. Could the guest be Captain Chadwell? Could he have returned. "Thank you, Nell. I shall come down directly."

Heart hammering, she looked in the mirror and pinched some color into her cheeks. She turned to the armoire. Surely she had a more flattering dress than this simple sprigged muslin. But she could not wait to see him. And if the guest was not the captain, there was no need to change. She turned to the bed and reached for an old shawl, whirled to the mirror again, and dissatisfied, tossed the shawl back on the bed.

Her hands shook as she opened the door and she fought for composure as she walked down the stairs. Before she reached the landing, her heart fell and she was overwhelmed with disappointment. The strident voice she heard was Lady Sedgewyck, none other.

She entered the drawing room and made her curtsy to both ladies. "Good afternoon, Lady Sedgewyck."

Henrietta turned and smiled briefly before plunging back into a detailed account of her latest shopping excursion.

After a stultifyingly dull ten minutes of monologue by Henrietta, Rosalind heard the doorknocker sound. Downstairs, Jaspers opened the door but she couldn't hear the exchange. A few minutes later, he appeared in the doorway.

He cleared his throat noisily, trying to end the chatter from Lady Sedgewyck. "A Mr. Oliver Thorne wishes to see you, Miss Elliott."

"Tell him to come up," Lady Rotherford said.

"Who is Mr. Thorne?" Henrietta's raspy whisper was loud enough to resound throughout the house.

"A gentleman I met at my friend Delphine's wedding."

"Mr. Thorne." Evers announced the name in a clear and dispassionate voice.

Mr. Thorne came into the room and bowed to Rosalind. "I hope I am not interrupting you ladies."

"Grandmother, may I make known to you Mr. Thorne? And, Lady Sedgewyck, my new acquaintance, Mr. Thorne."

Oliver bowed deeply to Lady Rotherford and Lady Sedgewyck.

"Please be seated, Mr. Thorne. When did you arrive in Bath?"

"I arrived last evening. I am putting up at the Royal York, a very comfortable establishment."

"Well situated, indeed," Lady Sedgewyck said. She looked back and forth between Rosalind and Oliver as if assessing the depth of their feelings.

"I was telling Lady Rotherford and Miss Elliott about my efforts to have a new mattress put into my house. You see, Mr. Thorne, I have just taken a house near here in the Royal Circus. My husband, the earl, is here to take the cure and he is unable to . . ."

Rosalind wondered how long it would take Mr. Thorne to glaze over at the boring nature of Henrietta's chatter. But a full ten minutes had ticked by on the mantel clock before Lady Sedgewyck completed her monologue. He had kept a look of interest on his face throughout her chattering and did not seem prepared to change the subject.

"What is the nature of your husband's affliction?"

Good heavens, Rosalind thought. Now Lady Sedgewyck would be off for another fifteen or twenty minutes of diagnosis. How could he have asked such a question? Couldn't he tell by the last soliloquy that she would not stop for anything?

Mr. Thorne was politely attentive to Lady Sedgewyck, whether from interest or good manners Rosalind could not tell.

Rosalind took the opportunity to look at him, nicely dressed in gray pantaloons with a tan waistcoat and blue jacket, entirely unremarkable and proper. His neckcloth was neatly tied in a simple knot with no flourishes of dandyism. She could find nothing to alter her opinion of propriety but neither had there ever been even a hint of spirit about the man. He was everything a woman was supposed to be looking for, of good birth, well educated, apparently not given to gaming or boisterous sport, polite and well mannered. Why was it she could not find him appealing?

As Henrietta prattled on, Evers brought the tea tray. Not until all of them had been served and Henrietta at last paused for a sip from her teacup did Lady Rotherford speak.

"My granddaughter reported that the wedding of Miss Epley and Mr. Sandborne was a lovely affair."

"Yes, a happy occasion, and particularly felicitous for me since I was able to meet Miss Elliott. The new Mrs. Sandborne has often praised your granddaughter to me, but until I actually was introduced, I had no idea how the praise actually fell short of reality."

Rosalind suppressed the laughter that threatened to engulf her. But Grandmother was obviously thrilled, her face wreathed in smiles.

Before she gathered her words, however, Lady Sedgewyck set down her teacup and resumed the center of attention. "Miss Elliott has been very kind to my daughter. She is an adorable little scamp, Charlotte is, and. . ."

Rosalind's suppressed laughter turned sour. If ever there was a mother who cared less for her child than Henrietta, she could not imagine it.

Lady Sedgewyck quickly turned to a recital of all the admirable qualities and not a few unsavory ones she found in Bath, pronouncing most of the entertainments to be tame. "I am organizing a little picnic day after tomorrow, Mr. Thorne. I hope you will be able to join our party."

Hardly waiting for his nod of assent, she prosed on about the difficulty of the arrangements, the river barges, the transportation of the victuals, the necessity of having perfect weather.

At last the mantel clock obliged by chiming the hour, even stirring Lady Sedgewyck to remark about the time and how she was never one to over-stay her welcome.

Which happened about three-quarters of an hour ago, Rosalind thought.

Grandmother rose as the parting pleasantries were drawn out to a ridiculous extent, as Mr. Thorne was re-welcomed to Bath, and re-invited to the picnic. Nods, bows, and more curtsies were ex-changed and at last Lady Sedgewyck waved her way out of the room, accompanied to the entrance by Lady Rotherford.

"You are looking in fine spirits, Miss Elliott."

What a clever remark, Rosalind thought, but then one could hardly expect brilliance after the mind-numbing conversation of the last hour. "Are you staying long in Bath, Mr. Thorne?" Rosalind cringed inwardly at her matching lack of wit.

"That depends. I have my rooms for a fortnight."

"I see." Rosalind watched Mr. Thorne sit up straighter, clear his throat, and act as though he was about to make a Momentous Declaration.

"The reason I called on you today, besides to meet your estimable grandmother, was to request your companionship on a little stroll later this af-ternoon. I have been reliably informed that the hour of four is the customary time for taking the air in the Parade. I should very much like to have you join me."

"I should be happy to take the air with you, Mr. Thorne." Curling up with her book sounded more inviting, but Rosalind felt she could hardly refuse his courtesy.

Lady Rotherford returned to her chair, somewhat winded from the climb back to the first floor. Rosalind was quite willing to allow the two others to take over the conversation.

Mr. Thorne commented on the handsome room, certainly one would call this the *piano nobile*, a fine room, proportions perfect and colors so very a la mode.

Lady Rotherford invited him to dine with them on the morrow and perhaps join them at the lower rooms if he found that to his taste.

He agreed to all, with the proper amount of appreciation, even deference. He took his departure, allowing that he would return for Rosalind in two hours.

Rosalind breathed a sigh of relief. Perhaps she could indulge in two hours of silence.

But Lady Rotherford was full of questions. "What about this young man, Rosalind? You never told me about him. While I was downstairs, I had to find Nell and ask her if he was well enough acquainted with you to be invited to dinner. Nell said you two had been practically inseparable at the wedding. And you never even mentioned his name. Am I to conclude you have no interest in him? Never say he is another fortune hunter!"

"Grandmother, I think you are taking elocution lessons from Lady Sedgewyck. The fact is I find Mr.

Thorne quite unexceptional. A pleasant gentleman perhaps but a bit of a dull dog."

"I did not find him dull in the least. He was all that is polite. What do you know of his family?"

"Nothing." Rosalind chose not to say anything more. If Lady Rotherford cared enough to make inquiries, there were probably dozens of people here in Bath who knew his pedigree and his situation as well.

Lady Rotherford frowned. "I can not imagine why you do not have an interest in Mr. Thorne. I am only sorry he arrived while Lady Sedgewyck was here. That woman talks incessantly. Do you think she was including us in her invitation to a picnic? Eating outdoors. Bah! What nonsense."

Philip came downstairs to the coffee room after a miserable night at the Bell and Anchor. The mattress must have been original to the fourteenth century inn, for it both sagged pitifully and was full of lumps.

When he could not sleep, he paced and thought about the house, how Miss Elliott would look in every room, excoriated himself for such foolish thoughts, and finished off a bottle of claret, its high quality hinting at a flourishing smuggler's trade nearby.

The land at Lymore Park was entirely in pasture, no crops having been planted for many years. Fertile, though, the men said, and excellent for barley and oats. There were plenty of local fellows who would be only too happy to have the work if Philip chose to put the fields into production again.

Now as he ate fried bread and a rasher of bacon,

Philip wondered how he might do as a farmer of sorts. His early childhood had been on land that bore many good crops, but he had not stayed there long enough to know anything more than the rudiments of ploughing and cultivating. Rigging a ship he knew about, all right, and he was familiar with life in a dozen ports from the channel to the Caribbean. Would he make a damn fool of himself if he tried to oversee fields?

But none of his musings cured his brain of the recurring image of a lovely young lady tending a garden restored to beauty and a drawing room turned from shabby to elegant.

There was no escaping the fact that he wanted Rosalind as his wife. It was a completely unfamiliar feeling; never before had he contemplated marriage in any but the most general way. And what of the image that also tickled the back of his mind, the image of children, a pair of brown-haired boys and a chubby blond girl, that wouldn't leave him alone?

As much as he despised the place, he would return to Bath tomorrow.

Sixteen

Rosalind tied the bow on her chip straw bonnet, picked up a shawl in case the weather turned cooler on the river, and grabbed a parasol for protection from the sun. She ought to be looking forward to the picnic, but even though the weather was fine, she could not summon any enthusiasm.

Ten days passed since she last had seen Captain Chadwell. As far as she knew, his name had faded from the gossipers' vocabularies, replaced perhaps by Mr. Thorne. For that, she ought to thank the solemn friend of Delphine's husband.

Mr. Thorne was attentive and solicitous, well read and intelligent, polite to a fault. He danced creditably, never trod on her toe or spilled a drop of punch on her gown. He knew a great deal about Mozart and enjoyed the historical plays of the Bard. He thoroughly charmed Grandmother and all her friends, who sought his company from mornings in the Pump Room to evenings in the Upper Rooms. He knew a wide variety of card games and never tried to excuse himself from a table of three elderly ladies.

Mr. Thorne met with everyone's approval except hers. Rosalind found him as lackluster a gentleman as she ever had known.

He had not yet made her an offer of marriage, but she knew he would be down on one knee before much more time passed. She honestly tried to give serious thought to marrying him. But it was hopeless. When she thought of Philip Chadwell, her heart sang and her pulse beat rapidly. When she thought of Oliver Thorne, she found herself yawning.

"Rosalind? If you do not hurry, we shall be tardy. The chairs have been waiting for a quarter hour already." Lady Rotherford's voice broke into her reverie.

Rosalind glanced in the mirror, shrugged, and went downstairs. She would have enjoyed walking to the river, but as Lady Rotherford preferred to be carried, they rode to the barge dock below the bridge.

The late June weather made up for cool weather in May. The sun shone brightly in a cloudless sky and a little breeze fluttered the leaves of the trees. A good thing, Rosalind thought. If raindrops threatened her fete, Henrietta would have exacted some major revenge on Mother Nature.

Once on the barges, they sat on cushioned benches and watched the passing shoreline. Soon they had left the town far behind and the tower of the Abbey soon disappeared as they rounded a bend. One of the attendants had to shoo a herd of cows out of the water ahead of them so that they could continue.

Lady Rotherford turned away from her conversation with Lady Isiline and whispered in Rosalind's ear. "Imagine how that Henrietta abuses her poor husband, not only dragging him and his feeble joints into the wilderness. Think what she does to his pocketbook. We are to have ices for dessert on a hot day along the river?"

"Imagine."

Lady Rotherford turned back to Lady Isiline for more of the atrocities she enjoyed hearing about the domineering ways of the obnoxious Countess of Sedgewyck.

All Rosalind wanted to hear about was the location of Captain Chadwell and his plans to return to Bath.

Eventually they reached the meadow Henrietta had chosen for her outdoor luncheon, already supplied with tents and tables and teeming with busy servants, the provisioners' wagons and horses, and musicians. Henrietta presided like a general positioning his troops for battle.

Rosalind and Mr. Thorne were assigned to play shuttlecock over a net set beside the river. They managed to hit the little clump of feathers back and forth several times before one of Mr. Thorne's swipes at the flying shuttlecock sent it smack into the water. It rapidly sailed downstream a few feet before sinking below the surface.

Mr. Thorne looked flustered. "Oh, my. I did not mean to hit it quite so vigorously."

Rosalind swallowed a bubble of laughter. Mr. Thorne was hardly the kind of man who appreciated the humor in his own conduct. "Surely there must be more shuttlecocks."

As she spoke, a footman in the Sedgewyck livery presented Mr. Thorne with another. The game resumed, only for him to lose another shuttlecock and then another.

Within half an hour, the music ended and Lord Sedgewyck asked them all to sit down.

Rosalind was warm and felt her hair drooping from the mild exertion. Mr. Thorne escorted her to the table under the tent and took a place across from her. "I fear I have not turned out to be much of a racquet man."

Rosalind spoke softly, hoping the elderly gentleman nearby was at least a little hard of hearing. "I think you did an admirable job. After all, I believe our main purpose was to occupy a place in the tableau Lady Sedgewyck prepared, something for the older folks to watch while they listened to the strings."

He tried to rearrange his wilted cravat. "Yes, I see your point."

Rosalind was about to help herself from a platter of chicken when she heard the unmistakable pounding of hooves in the distance. Her heightened pulse revealed the way in which her mind jumped to the same conclusion every time a door was knocked upon or a carriage rolled through the street. Could this be Philip returning?

Putting the thought out of her mind, she helped herself to a cutlet.

Moments later, she nearly dropped her fork when she heard the unmistakable voice of Captain Chadwell greeting his father and stepmother.

"Ah, my boy," the earl said. "Glad to see you back."

Captain Chadwell made his greetings to his great-aunt and several other persons at the other end of the table.

Rosalind's heart thudded as she looked at him. She had so much she wanted to say, so many apologies to make, so many notions spinning in her head. She sipped her wine, watching the goblet tremble in her unsteady hand.

After the rude manner in which she had last spoken to him, Captain Chadwell would be entirely justified in disregarding her absolutely. And if he did? She set down the glass and clenched her fists to steady them. Why, she could call on Lady Isiline. Or ask Fanny to invite him to her house. Or hide in a passageway and confront him on the street. Somehow she would make her request for his pardon.

Eventually, when Rosalind thought her nerves would snap under the strain, Captain Chadwell came to her end of the table and greeted her warmly. She could hardly believe her ears.

Across the table, Mr. Throne stood, waiting to be introduced.

Rosalind stuttered a little as she introduced the gentlemen. "Captain, m—may I make known to you Mr. Oliver Thorne. Mr. Thorne, Captain Chadwell is Lady Sedgewyck's stepson."

"Good afternoon."

One of the footmen brought a chair and the captain sat down next to Rosalind. She clasped her hands in her lap to hide their shaking and tried to calm her racing pulse.

"Are you a navy man?" Mr. Thorne asked.

"I was."

"Captain Chadwell was the master of *H. M. S. Venture* until last year," Rosalind said.

"I once longed to be a navy man." Mr. Thorne addressed Captain Chadwell in his usual grave tone. "It is fortunate I never got my wish, because I recently crossed the Irish Sea and had a wretched case of mal de mer on my way and worse on the return."

Captain Chadwell chuckled. "Seasickness is no

stranger to the navy. If a man has never been sea-
sick, he simply has not been long enough at sea."

Philip waved away the waiters with dish after dish.
The only hunger he had was to be alone with Rosalind, away from all the people. He knew what he
wanted to say. All he needed was the chance, and
now that he sat in her presence, he could afford to
be patient.

When he had arrived in Bath a few hours ago, he
had gone directly to the Royal Crescent to find Miss
Elliott, intending to waste no time in asking for her
hand in marriage. He had thought out his plan of
battle carefully. A frontal assault by stating his desire to make her his wife, without allowing her to
answer him until he completed two flanking ma-
neuvers. In one, he would confess the source of his
bad reputation and confirm his reform. The other
flank would be a bit more tricky. He wanted her to
know that he could keep her in comfort if not
splendor. Bragging was not his forte and he did not
want to overstate his case. But he wanted her to
know she was not marrying a poor man.

When Lady Rotherford's butler had told him the
ladies were not at home, he added they were on a
picnic outing with Lady Isiline. When Philip went
to his former residence, only Charlotte was home
with the servants and a very unhappy Charlotte she
had been.

"They left without me. Mama refused to take me.
She said I would not sit still on the boat while they
sailed to the meadow. But I would have. I am not a
baby. They are having raspberry ice, my very favorite." She had stamped her little feet and raged.

"Where have they gone?" he asked the pouting child.

But she did not know and could not describe the place. Philip promised her two raspberry ices to-morrow and her very own picnic soon.

Downstairs in the kitchen, only the scullery maid remained. She knew little except that the men from Davis's were supplying the food.

Philip had rushed to Davis & Co. where a harried manager at last was able to draw him a map. The place was not far by horseback, for the river curved and meandered through the countryside. What would take an hour by barge could take a horse cross-country about half that time.

But they had a long start on him, and when he finally found the place, the meal was already underway.

Now here he sat, waiting good-naturedly for the chance to stroll along the river with Miss Elliott. But who was this Mr. Thorne, this jackanapes dressed like fashion plate for picnic attendees? Philip fought off a stab of jealousy. He had a strategy and he could not allow the green-eyed monster to interfere.

Miss Elliott kept her gaze on her plate, as though studying her food.

"I thought sailors learned to overcome seasickness," Mr. Thorne said.

"On most voyages, that is true. But when the weather blows in, some who brag they never feel queasy are forced to take back their boasts."

Miss Elliott looked at him with a shy little smile. "You were away from Bath, Captain Chadwell?"

He wished he could reach over and plant a kiss on those curving lips. "I visited some old friends in

Portsmouth." Which was entirely correct as far as it went. "How was your friend's wedding?"

"Very fine in every way."

Mr. Thorne nodded. "Miss Elliott is the best friend of the bride and I am the best friend of the groom."

So that explained it. Not hard to imagine how he might have been smitten by Rosalind. Not hard at all.

Captain Chadwell began to fume as they made small talk, of the weather, the cloudless sky, the song of the meadowlarks, the wild roses that spilled over the fallen tree trunk. The prospect of rain was examined and found likely tomorrow. The conversation was wearisome, but he held up his part.

A passing boat, rowed by a young man and sitting low in the water under the weight of a large barrel, was compared to various aquatic crafts in innumerable lakes, ponds, and rivers. When that subject was exhausted, they spoke about the relative merits of calf versus kidskin.

"For suppleness," Mr. Thorne said, "I find kidskin superior in articles such as gloves."

Philip was amazed that Rosalind had not emptied her glass of wine over Mr. Thorne's head. Or his. She added little to the discussion. Philip saw it as a challenge to best the younger man at his own game. Even the most simple and prosaic of topics could be stretched into a conversation that scrutinized more implications, complications, and inferences than Henrietta's emeralds had facets. Mr. Thorne expressed his opinions with only the mildest of differences so politely put in such a deferential manner that no one could object.

Rosalind continued to pick at her food, while

Philip ate nothing, keeping himself in fighting trim for the verbal jousting.

The value of sea-bathing was compared to taking the waters in Bath. The efficacy of a new cure for gout, espoused by a German doctor, could not have been so highly recommended if some suffering had not been relieved.

When at last the conversation devolved into the habits of bees, Philip felt he was on the verge of a final parry and killing thrust.

Mr. Thorne was positive in his opinion. "I find the honey made from hives in fields of clover superior to any others."

Captain Chadwell moved in for his coup de grâce. "Then I assume you have not tasted the honey made from orange blossoms in the tropics. The color is pale amber; the body and aroma are outstanding. If you ever have the opportunity to taste it, you will be amazed."

Mr. Thorne seemed to concede. "I shall endeavor to try your recommendation."

At last people were beginning to leave the table and the musicians tuned up for more music.

Mr. Thorne stood and bowed to Miss Elliott. "Excuse me for a moment. I shall return after I have a word with Lady Sedgewyck."

Rosalind smiled and nodded.

Philip watched Mr. Thorne move out of hearing before he spoke. "If he thinks a moment will suffice for words with Henrietta, he does not know the lady very well."

"I would say they are two of a kind, Captain."

Philip grinned. "Miss Elliott, I have put up with that silly young ass for the past hour in the hopes of speaking with you in private. I am not accustomed to his kind of conversation over nothing. But to match him to Henrietta? This is indeed slander."

He wished he could decipher her enigmatic smile.

Philip had only one question that mattered before he began his well-thought-out campaign. "May I ask you, do you care for him?"

"Mr. Thorne is a very proper young man."

"But do you welcome his attentions? I do not know the proper way to ask this. Does he hold a place high in your affections?"

"No. He does not, Captain Chadwell." She looked away shyly.

"Would you take a stroll with me along the river?"

Her face lit up with pleasure. "Oh, yes. I have been hoping to speak with you too . . ."

"Then take my arm, and we shall give the ladies a little excitement to interfere with their digestion."

She laughed out loud, the kind of happy laugh he loved to hear from her, the kind he wanted to hear for years to come.

They walked through the long grass to the path alongside the water. A few puffy clouds dotted the sky and a kestrel circled in the distance. From a clump of trees came the trill of the nuthatch, a familiar childhood sound Philip was surprised to recall. When they were around the bend and out of sight of the picnic, he drew a deep breath and halted, taking her hand and turning her to face him.

"Rosalind, I came back to Bath because you are here. You have been prominent in my thoughts every day and every night. I wish to have you as my wife, Rosalind."

She opened her mouth but he touched a finger to her lips. Her parasol fell unheeded to the ground.

"No, please do not say anything until you have

heard all that I have to say. Before you make a judgment on my suit, I need to explain several things. You have heard the gossip about me. You know that I did some very foolish things as a young man. I found my disgrace was a blessing in disguise, as the saying goes."

"How so?"

"People heard about me and they pretended to be shocked. That relieved me of many uncomfortable duties. 'Ah, he is pockets-to-let and a despicable rogue to boot,' they say. 'Not suitable for polite company.'

"You cannot overestimate how convenient that has been for me. It has saved me untold hours of tiresome company at tedious gatherings."

"Captain Chadwell, I begin to see you as a misanthrope."

"Perhaps I am. Or rather, was. You see, I never thought to wish myself suitable for the good graces of a lady such as you. So I let my reputation stand, however inflated it was. My youthful indiscretions, I assure you, were highly exaggerated and never repeated."

He paused. A meadowlark resumed its song in the distance. Rosalind held herself very stiff, as if afraid to brush against him. He really wanted to ditch the rest of his speech and kiss her immediately. But he went on.

"Miss Elliott, do you find my reputation a barrier to our, ah, friendship? Do you hold me in scorn, despise me because I have had a scandal in my past."

"It was ten years ago?"

"More than a dozen. But like so many old scandals, it is dredged up from time to time and embellished almost beyond recognition."

"Those old stories do not concern me."

"Good. The other part of my reputation is equally untrue. I am generally regarded as without wealth. That assumption is in error. I have never publicized the fact, but I took several prizes and managed to put away some funds while I commanded the *Venture*."

"You mean you are not a fortune hunter? You were not after Lady Isiline's money?"

Shock shot through him like a scimitar. "Is that what people said?"

"Yes, that you brought her to Bath in order to be the primary beneficiary of her will."

"What the devil! And what did people expect she would leave her own children? Nothing?" His anger grew by the second.

"I do not know."

"Blast and damn, excuse me, Miss Elliott. Those gossips are bloodsuckers."

"Yes, many are."

He fought to damp down his fury. "I expected everyone to think I was poor, but I had no idea anyone would think I was after Aunt Izzy's money."

For a moment he stared past her shoulder at the river, willing away his resentment. At last he took a deep breath and went on. "Excuse me. I never thought . . . Miss Elliott, I have never disclosed this to another person with the exception of my man of business and my solicitor. Without in any way trying to enhance my standing, I can tell you I have a handsome sum gained from my naval days, invested well, with a yearly income of several thousand pounds if I choose to take it. Otherwise, my instructions are that it be put into other worthy projects with a reasonable income to be expected.

I have always valued my privacy. I never cared what others thought of my financial ability or lack of it.

"I tell you this not to boast, but to assure you of my sincerity in declaring my affections for you. I am not a fortune hunter. When I confessed my feelings for you, I did not care for a moment how much money you have, nor how many estates."

Rosalind smiled and nodded. "I believe you, Philip."

"Rosalind, what I most wanted to tell you is that I have been away from Bath looking for property. I found a small estate near the channel. I have made a tentative purchase, with the understanding that it must meet my bride's approval."

"What?"

"If you will marry me, Miss Elliott, I will take you there to see it. If you do not like the property, we will look elsewhere."

"But I . . ."

He stopped and pulled her into his arms. "I have been talking more than that fellow back there. Or Henrietta, deuce take it. Now I am ready for your answer."

Rosalind felt the tears well into her eyes. "Yes, Captain, I will marry you."

He kissed her, good and hard and thoroughly. "I want you to live with me in our own house, be my wife and perhaps the mother of my children, and share the rest of our lives. Unless, that is"—he laughed a little—"you suffer from seasickness and prefer to remain on land when I go out to sail."

Rosalind listened to him as if in a dreamworld. This was better than any of the fantasies she had woven over the past few weeks. She felt as if she had not a bone or muscle in her body. She was a formless mass of cotton stuffing, molding herself to his strength.

She managed to whisper against his chest. "I am so sorry. I should not have believed you were a fortune hunter even for a moment."

"I am not easily offended, you know."

"And I apologize for almost giving you the cut direct in the Pump Room."

His laughter was muffled against her hair. "I love you. I only hope you can bear to be married to a man everyone else thinks is a rogue."

"None of that matters to me. I can forgive you your past if you can forgive me for doing nothing with my life. You have seen the world. I have seen Bath. You have sailed the oceans, fought daring battles. I have taken tea with elderly ladies, danced with old gentlemen so rickety they could hardly stand."

"You do not care what anyone thinks?"

"I shall simply tell them the truth. I am in love with you and nothing else matters."

"And do you expect everyone to believe you?

Rosalind sighed. "For the moment, I don't care a fig."

"Shall we hurry back and tell the rest or should we keep it a secret between us for the moment?"

"A secret, please. I do not want to be subjected to a lecture on weddings by Henrietta and neither do you."

"How very perceptive you are, my darling." He tipped up her chin with his thumb and brushed his lips across hers.

"Tell me about the house." She spoke with her mouth pressed to his, her veins afire, melting the center of her being.

"It is old, built of stone over many centuries. Roofs

and chimneys all higgledy-piggledy. In need of a lady's hand."

"Are there old diamond-paned windows? And oak-beamed ceilings?"

He dipped his mouth into the hollow between her neck and shoulder. "Oh, by all means. Especially in the principal bedchamber."

Her response was lost in his kiss, but never missed.

Seventeen

Philip rode home slowly, lost in thought. If he had been on a less well-traveled road, he would have talked out loud to Neptune. The animal had shown himself to be a sympathetic listener.

He tried to remember all he had said to Rosalind. Had he explained everything? He felt sure he had forgotten some of what he wanted to tell her. Important things. Inconsequential things. The name of the estate, for example.

So he had been considered a fortune hunter here in Bath, dangling after a piece of his great-aunt's fortune. Irritating and despicable. How could people have thought that of him? Was even Admiral Gladfeller aware of the charges?

And suddenly the ghastly truth hit him like a belaying pin between his shoulders. When they announced their betrothal, everyone in Bath would think he was marrying Miss Elliott for her money. The force of the shocking realization left him breathless.

The damnable wretches who spent their lives spoiling the interests of others. Fools and idiots alike. Some hunted like lions, stalking and extinguishing their prey. And the rest of them were like a pack of hungry hyenas waiting to pounce on the carcass after the lions ate their fill. Yes, both lions and hyenas lived here in droves.

He carefully shepherded his funds so that no one would know their extent. His degree of wealth was no one's business but his own. He wasn't fond of being thought a near-pauper, however, a man who would toad-eat his own relatives trying to cheat his cousins out of their rightful inheritance.

Well, what did he care? Not that some called him a libertine. He didn't care that people thought he had stolen away with another man's wife. He didn't care that all of it was only half true.

But it was no longer just his business, was it? He might not care if he was thought to be a fortune hunter, but the thought of people talking of Miss Elliott as the victim of a fortune hunter? Abominable indeed. And not to be tolerated for a moment.

As Neptune meandered along the road, a cart full of happy villagers passed by laughing and singing. It was an old sea chanty, one he had often heard his men sing. Perhaps some of the men were like himself, home from the long years of war at sea, looking for a new life.

"Way, haul away, we'll haul for fair weather,

"Way, haul away, we'll haul away home . . ."

Until the song faded into the distance, Philip felt the strong ache of memories, both good and bad, of the life he had left behind. Nostalgia for a life he had loved at times and despised at others. At least things had been simpler. Right versus wrong. Good versus bad. Now everything had twists and turns, confusing shadows everywhere.

Rosalind Elliott, gentle, sweet, and all that was

perfect in a woman. He could not imagine his life without her.

But was it fair of him to tar her with the brush of his reputation? She might not care about his old rakish reputation, but others would talk of it. She claimed it made no difference to her, all over a long time ago. And he believed her when she said she would not hold his past against him if he did not hold her past against her, her past being so colorless and uninteresting compared to his sea exploits. Yes, he truly believed her.

But how would she react in a dozen years when people still said, "Oh poor Rosalind Elliott, that man married her for her money." No matter what he did or she said, would not people remember him primarily as a fortune hunter and her as his victim?

Suddenly the beautiful sunny day seemed dark, the motion of the horse as steeply rolling as the tossing of a ship on a stormy sea, the very air pressing down so that he could hardly take a breath.

What had he done? He had opened her to the criticism of those with whom she had always lived and those she loved. It was the action of a cad, of a bounder, of a witless wretch who had not thought through his battle plan beyond the victory to the peace. In years to come, when she visited her grandmother here in Bath—God forbid he should ever have to see the city again—everyone would call her poor Mrs. Chadwell, wasting her money on that wastrel, that worthless fool.

Abruptly he kicked Neptune into a canter. He needed to be back at the Royal Crescent before Rosalind and Lady Rotherford arrived home. He had to be there to withdraw his offer of marriage before anyone besides he and Rosalind knew of his proposal.

From the sedan chair, Rosalind saw Philip waiting for them, pacing up and down in front of the gently curved facade. She longed to get out and run to him, let him hold her tight and swing her around in a great arc. But instead of a pleasant anticipatory smile, his face was a cold mask. What had happened in the last hour and a half? Panic gripped her in its cold grasp.

When they were inside, he greeted her grandmother as though it were just any day, commenting briefly on the picnic until Lady Rotherford went upstairs to attend to the barking of Pip and Popsy.

Though Rosalind willed his eyes to meet hers, his gaze remained steadfastly on the marble floor. Neither spoke until they heard Lady Rotherford cooing to the spaniels from the Rose Salon.

"What is wrong, Philip?" Rosalind asked.

Hardly a muscle moved in his face. "I fear I have been selfish and impulsive. I did not consider what disapprobation would fall upon your name if it was to be linked to mine."

"Whatever are you talking of, Captain?"

"I feel certain people will pity you when they hear you are betrothed to me. I cannot have that happen. Please consider my remarks at the riverside to have been the delusions of a selfish and monstrous villain. I had no right to ask you to be my wife. I am not worthy of you, and I will not allow you to become an object of great pity in the eyes of your friends."

"I ask again, Philip, what nonsense is this of which you speak?"

"I was impulsive. I did not think through the consequences of our betrothal. As I said, people will think you are the victim of a fortune hunter. They will pity you and shake their heads in compassion and sympathy for your poor plight."

"And what do you take me for? When have I ever indicated to you that I cared a whit for the gossip of others? And to let the potential opinions of other people affect my happiness? I am not such a poor creature, I assure you."

"But if everyone thinks I am a fortune hunter? You will then be my prey."

He looked so worried, so concerned she almost giggled. "You believed me, I think, when I said I cared nothing for your ancient misdeeds. Why can you not believe me when I say I am not concerned about any charges of fortune hunting on your part?"

"When a woman chooses a man to marry of her own free will, they will be two beings in a partnership based on love and affection, not arranged by anyone else. But what of the possibility that the woman is duped into marriage, wooed by a cad who sweeps her away and makes her fortune his own. She is an object of pity. I cannot let it happen to you, Rosalind. You enjoy a position of respect. That I cannot sully. You will meet a man someday who is worthy of you in all regards. Even your Mr. Thorne, perhaps."

"Philip Chadwell, did you stop on the way back from the picnic and down a bottle of spirits? You are talking like your sense has gone missing."

"I have never been more sober nor more serious

in my life. I made a terrible error, Rosalind, but it is not too late. I am rescinding my offer of marriage."

The sincerity of his words finally sank in. She could hardly speak for the huge lump in her throat and her eyes burned with tears. "Think of my feelings, Philip. I feared you were gone forever. Now you return and propose marriage. I am the happiest of females for about one hour. Then you find some trumped-up reason to withdraw the proposal. I call that a scam hardly worthy of a man of honor. And then to tell me your thoughts are based on what gossips will say in the Pump Room when I know how little you care for anything they say!"

Rosalind was practically shouting by the time she broke down and burst into tears.

He came to her and touched her shoulder. She shook him off and searched in her reticule for a handkerchief. The scrap of lace she found was entirely inadequate for the job. She collapsed on the bottom step of the staircase and pulled out the hem of her petticoat to catch the tears.

Lady Rotherford looked over the railing from two floors up. "What is going on down there? I may not have the most acute hearing in the world, but I would say you are either arguing or crying, Rosalind."

"Both," she whispered through her tears. She coughed, then stood up again. "No, Grandmother," she called. "We are merely talking about the picnic."

"Come up here and tell me what you are saying."

"In a few moments, Grandmother." She smoothed her gown over the damp spot on her petticoat and sniffed. "I am sorry. I do not often indulge in waterworks."

"I do not wish to upset you."

Her tears had turned to white-hot anger. Her words were clipped, her tone stern. "You certainly have upset me. I very much want to marry you, Philip. I am not a green miss who is afraid of her shadow. Or afraid of her shadow's reputation."

"I cannot allow it. Besmirching your reputation, Rosalind? It is not possible."

"Philip Chadwell, you are a blasted hypocrite! I accepted your proposal. And now you are trying to get out of it."

"But—"

"Just say it. Say you wanted to marry me an hour ago. But now you have changed your mind. Say you do not wish to marry me."

"Ah, Rosalind. I do not know what to say."

"Tell me you want to marry me. Tell me you do not want to live without me. For that is the way I feel about you, Philip."

"I love you. I love you. But I love you too much to see you unhappy and upset, the respect you enjoy in ruins."

Grandmother leaned over the railing again. "If you do not come up here immediately, Rosalind and Captain Chadwell, I shall come down. And I will hold you responsible for the damage to my poor limbs."

He opened the front door and stepped outside. "Good-bye, Rosalind."

The door slammed on her anguished cry.

Rosalind lay on the chaise in her grandmother's boudoir, tears running into her hair. She no longer bothered to wipe them away.

What had he said? That she was respected by

everyone in Bath, they found her a worthy young woman. If she accepted his proposal, she would lose her good standing, be lowered in everyone's eyes, a laughingstock. To Rosalind none of that mattered. But he was gone again, a martyr to her silly reputation.

"Have some of your tea, my dear." Lady Rotherford wiped a tear off her own cheek. "I cannot bear seeing you so distressed."

"I cannot pretend to be anything but miserable, Grandmother. I love him. And he loves me. But he will not have me because of my infernal money. Oh, why is it so awful to marry a woman with money?"

"Perhaps it is for the best, Rosalind."

"Oh no," she moaned. "Never say so. He is the best of men." She sat up and brushed the damp strands of hair away from her face.

"Grandmother, you do not understand. He is not marrying me for my money. He has plenty of his own. And as for that old story about running off to Paris with that woman, he was hardly more than a boy. Other men might have flaunted their reputations, had a series of affairs with great London ladies, become a celebrated rake. Look at the behavior tolerated among the *haute ton,* people who have not honored their marriage vows for years and years."

"I do not disagree, my dear. Moral standards have fallen precipitously."

"Even the royal princes . . ."

"Do not mention them, those Hanoverians!"

Rosalind could not help smiling through her tears. "He told me Lady DeMuth was only looking for someone to take her to Paris. She took advantage of his youth and vulnerability."

"You spoke of it with him?"

"I did."

Lady Rotherford's eyes bulged almost as much as her spaniels'. "Rosalind, how could you?"

"He wanted to tell me the truth, to peel away all the layers of innuendo added over the years."

Lady Rotherford gulped her tea.

"It was a long time ago, Grandmother. Why should I care about what he did in 1802 when I was twelve years of age?"

"In my day we never would have mentioned such subjects."

Rosalind shook her head. "Perhaps not directly. But have I not heard you and your friends say a reformed rake makes a good husband?"

"Rosalind! Such things were never meant for your ears."

"You see, there is part of the problem!" Rosalind dried her eyes on a tea napkin and walked to the window. "Everyone, including Philip, thinks I am so delicate, so refined."

"As your mother was before you."

Rosalind paced up and down the carpet. "In Philip's eyes, I must seem a pathetic thing with no spine. He sees that I love Bath, our quiet life. I associate with the older ladies and gentlemen. I have no excitement about me. Why would he really care for me? I must seem faded and insipid. I am ordinary and boring. He has sailed all over the world."

She stopped and stared at the sleeping spaniels. "Grandmother, I will not let him go."

"My dear, if you truly love him, then I would never

stand in your way. In fact, I believe Lady Isiline and I would do anything we could to help you."

Lost in thought, Rosalind did not answer immediately. She knew there must be a way around his foolish objection. She would not sit back and let him drift away leaving them both alone to wash up on the shore, aground and isolated.

She sat down again. "I need to find a way . . ."

Popsy, now wide awake, hopped into her arms. Rosalind caressed the silky chestnut ears. "I wish I were like you, sweet Popsy. You truly do not care a fig what anyone thinks of you."

Pip occupied his favorite spot on Lady Rotherford's lap. "There, my sweet boy, can you chase Captain Chadwell and make him return?"

Rosalind knew her reputation as a rich woman. Perhaps it was time to end that impression. "Grandmother, I have an idea. No one knows where my money is invested. Remember last February, there was a bank which failed right here in Bath, the Bridgenorth Old Bank, and then Mr. Rowton's Bank closed to prevent a run? I am quite sure I had much of my fortune invested there. The losses must have been awful."

"Gracious no, dear, you said nothing . . . oh! You mean—"

"Why not? It is not as if I really would lose any money. And even if people think I have lost my investments, they know I own Fosswell Manor. No one will shed a tear for poor me." Rosalind gave a little laugh. "In fact, I imagine my reverses will come as good news to some people, especially those old misanthropes who think women should own nothing."

Lady Rotherford looked puzzled. "But it will

make you look foolish because you have made bad investments."

"No, Grandmother, my trustees make the investments. They would be the ones responsible for my losses. Actually I am lucky to have gentlemen of business who consult me on all major decisions. But, under Father's will, they are not so obliged. And no one knows what kind of relationship we have."

"If this is what you want to do, Rosalind, I will do what I can. In truth, I have become rather fond of Captain Chadwell myself."

When he regained awareness, Philip was not sure which was worse. His head throbbed, his back bent in an excruciating curl, his stomach roiled with sour bile, and his nose seemed buried in manure. He forced open his eyes and shoved himself to a sitting position, groaning with the pain of movement. A soft muzzle snuffled against his shoulder. Devil take it, he was sharing his straw bed with Neptune. How in the deuce had he ended up here? In the faint light of dawn, he could see the brandy bottle lying near his feet. He grasped the feed trough and hauled himself to his feet, staggering stiffly before he got his balance.

The horse nosed him again, as if asking what brought his master to such a state. Philip held on to the trough with one hand and scratched Neptune's ears with the other. "Thanks for not stepping on me, old boy."

He brushed the clinging straw from his clothes. From the looks of the growing brightness outside, he would have to hurry to be home before the streets were full of people.

Every step was a different kind of agony. But at last he managed to let himself in and make it to his bed before collapsing all over again.

He had no idea what hour it was by the time Gar wakened him.

"Blast it, I have slept until two in the afternoon."

"This is the third time I have tried to rouse you, Captain."

Philip sighed. "I had a late night."

"May I bring you a bath, sir?"

Philip knew he smelled as though he had slept in a stable. After all, that was exactly what he had done. "Yes. And whatever remedy you can concoct for a devil of a head."

Unless Philip was mistaken, Gar had been almost laughing out loud when he left the room. But there was nothing funny about it.

An hour later, shaved, bathed, and dosed with some foul concoction, he felt almost human once again. But a human drowning in a sea of despair. His binge last evening had brought him nothing but a nightmarish delay in feeling the depths of his sorrow. Nothing had changed. The pain was every bit as intense.

He slumped in his chair, his stomach still rebelling at the thought of food. He probably could use some fresh air, but he could not bring himself to get up.

Gar came to the door again. "Captain?"

"Now what?"

"Miss Elliott has come to call."

He could not prevent the groan he uttered. "Can you tell her I am away from home?"

"No, sir. She and Lady Rotherford are with your great aunt in the drawing room. Lady Isiline told them you were upstairs."

Philip's head began to throb again. "I suppose you must tell them I will be down."

"Thank you, Captain."

When Gar was gone, Philip wiped his face with a damp cloth. How could he look at her again? How could he stop himself from taking her in his arms?

He knew he had hurt her. He had left her in tears yesterday. If she had a horse pistol downstairs with which to shoot him, he would not blame her. Please, just do not let her be crying again. That he could not stand.

When he walked into the drawing room, he felt he faced a court marshal for dereliction of duty. He could not bear to look at Rosalind and kept his gaze on the carpet.

"Good afternoon, ladies." His voice was hardly more than a mumble.

"Sit down, Philip," Lady Isiline said. "Miss Elliott has a plan."

He took a chair and stole a look at Rosalind. To his amazement, she looked as bright as a newly minted penny. "What is that?"

"I have a plan, Philip. A plan to appease your silly conscience and save my precious reputation."

"I do not understand."

"Philip, you said people think you are nearly a pauper. But what does Bath love more than a good new story?"

"Go on."

"I suggest you ask your friend Admiral Gladfeller to report on a letter he received asking after you and reporting your good luck in leaving the navy with such a handsome fortune gained in many feats of tremendous heroism."

"How will anyone believe such a story?"

"Why should they not believe it? All Bath loves a new *on-dit*. And with the rapidity news spreads here, before the week is out, you will have lines of supplicants at your door, begging for loans and gifts. In fact, if you were to endow a fund for the schooling of worthy young boys . . ."

Philip rubbed his hand over his eyes. Had he lost his mind or did this make some sense? "Rosalind, you are indeed a schemer of the first order."

"You have not heard it all yet. My plan has another little ploy to set up. We will entrust Grandmother and Lady Isiline with the sad story that my trustees report a great loss in my investments."

"What?" Philip was truly astonished.

"Why not? I shall be devastated at the news. Remember that bank that failed last winter? And was there not a story in the London papers from last week that told of a canal scheme that went awry? People lose money on all sorts of plans. All it will take is a bit of study to ascertain which projects have recently crashed."

Philip's head began to clear. "Pardon me for being slow, but this is a great deal to absorb. I am to become the wealthy one and you the pauper?"

Lady Isiline set down her teacup. "It seems to me that the two of you can work together just as you did to reunite Anne and me."

"And we shall help," Lady Rotherford added.

Rosalind looked from one to the other with fondness. "Grandmother is right. We managed to conquer their feud, so we should be able, if we work together, to find a way using the gossip itself?"

"We will start rumors?" Philip began to feel a glimmer of hope.

"Exactly," Rosalind said. "Once someone says you have a comfortable income, the next will say it is a fine fortune. Soon you will be one of the richest men in the realm."

"But you can not just start a story like that, can you?" Philip asked.

"Why not? Does Admiral Gladfeller know of your prize money?"

"No, I do not believe he does."

Lady Rotherford spoke again. "It is not unusual for men to have made handsome amounts in the navy, correct?"

"Not unusual," Philip answered. "But many naval men receive very little. Others have much more than I do."

"So tell Admiral Gladfeller," Lady Isiline said, "a little about your prize money. Make sure it is over-heard. That way it will spread even faster."

"What about Henrietta?" asked Lady Rotherford.

"She is only interested in talking about herself. But she might boast about her stepson's good fortune. And no doubt she will say she had known about it all along." Lady Isiline laughed so hard she almost upset her teacup.

Philip managed a smile. "If I were a wagering man, I would take that bet in a moment."

Rosalind walked over and placed her hand on his shoulder. "So you will, in the eyes of all of Bath, become quite the man of property. And, Grandmother, he actually purchased an estate in Devon. Philip, you must tell her all about it."

"Yes, Philip," Lady Isiline said. "We want to hear about your property."

Philip placed his hand over Rosalind's and told them about Lymore Park, the village, the church, the old house.

"Does it not sound wonderful?" Rosalind exclaimed when he was finished. "I will not mind losing most of my assets if I can live in such a place. In fact, I will enjoy no longer being an heiress."

"Never say you would want such a thing!" Lady Rotherford sounded aghast at the thought.

"Of course I do not. But I can say I have lost a great deal. I will let it be known in which collapsing funds I was invested."

Philip felt a twinge of caution. "Rosalind, are you sure you want to go that far?"

"Why not? Then when you marry me, people will pity you as the victim of a fortune-hunting female."

"That is ridiculous," he said.

"I do not think so. It will take only a short time for the stories to circulate. Meanwhile, you may dance with me once tomorrow evening at the Upper Rooms and I shall take two sets with Mr. Thorne. He will be very sympathetic to my losses. And I may even be able to shed a few tears again by then. Discreetly, but within view of a select few."

"You mean I have to attend one of those purgatories again?"

"Philip, we all heard you admit you enjoyed the last one, in spite of your attempt to find it dull. The evening will be even more amusing if we are manipulating the stories instead of being manipulated by them."

Philip had to admit the plan was worth trying. "Miss Rosalind Elliott, you are made for intrigue. Why the war office did not engage you to plan strategy I shall never understand."

Lady Rotherford nodded, her lace cap flapping in her excitement. "Isiline and I can do wonders. She is a master of the insinuation and allusion. She will be a strong ally."

Lady Isiline agreed. "Anne and I will do our very best tomorrow morning. You may be assured that no one will be in doubt as to her disappointment. I shall pretend to know nothing until Anne confides the sad story. As for Philip's tale, once the admiral tells a friend or two, we can count on Henrietta to trumpet the news throughout Bath. Rosalind, your plan will succeed splendidly."

Philip could not hold back his laughter. "I have rarely heard of someone so adept at turning the questionable qualities of society back upon itself. Rosalind, I admit I have underestimated your cunning up to now. Not only does your fortune probably outweigh mine, your cleverness leaves my poor brainbox far behind."

"Now, Anne," Lady Isiline said, "I think it is time to leave these two young people alone. They might have things to say to each other they don't want our old ears to hear."

Lady Rotherford smiled at Rosalind as she left the room. "I'll be ready to go home in about a half hour. Is that long enough for you?"

"Yes, thank you, Grandmother."

Philip stood and bowed them out of the room, then sat on the sofa, drawing Rosalind down beside him.

He caressed her cheek.

"So you will use the gossips against themselves, my lovely Miss Elliott?

"I certainly will if it means we can be married."

He took her into his arms and kissed her cheek,

her forehead. "You are the commander of this battle, my darling. The fleet will rally to your cause."

"I do wish you would stop talking and wasting our time alone." Rosalind pulled his head to hers and crushed her lips against his.

Eighteen

By the next evening's gathering at the Upper Rooms, the insinuations and hints dropped only that morning in the Pump Room had grown to prime topics of conversation, Rosalind was delighted to discover. She wore her gown of jonquil yellow, a color she loved but should never wear, for it gave her complexion a decidedly greenish cast. For tonight, it was the ideal ensemble.

"How are you, my dear," Lady Greyson asked, her voice dripping with *faux* pity. "I hope you are keeping your spirits high."

"Yes, I am trying." Rosalind could hardly keep from giggling.

Mr. Thorne was so solicitous she knew he must have heard about her misfortune, though he politely did not mention the calamity. Nor did her other dancing partners.

Strangely, everyone misinterpreted her silly grin, regenerated every time she caught sight of Captain Chadwell. People thought she was trying very hard to give the lie to her calamitous losses. The silly grin engendered a great deal of sympathy from assorted matrons, retired officers, and country nabobs.

Which merely caused Miss Elliott to grin even more.

Lady Sedgewyck hardly devoted a word to the sad story of Miss Elliott. Henrietta was much too eager to ply everyone with the immensity of dear Philip's heroism.

Rosalind was relieved when her grandmother suggested an early departure. She took one last glance at Captain Chadwell, in the center of a group with Admiral Gladfeller in the card room. He looked, she was relieved to see, quite comfortable.

Once home and comfortably ensconced in Lady Rotherford's Rose Room, Rosalind and Lady Rotherford compared notes, laughing so hard they actually frightened Popsy, who cowered under the sofa until they went up to bed.

The next morning, Rosalind and Lady Rotherford avoided the Pump Room and stayed home. Though they churned with curiosity about how the story was spreading, both ladies knew they soon would be well informed. Henrietta, Lady Sedgewyck was their first caller and bursting with news.

"My dears," she whispered. "I am so very sorry to report that the Pump Room was positively abuzz with your sad story. Rosalind, people were so very kind and sympathetic. I assured them that you were not quite to the point of requiring donations of foodstuffs. And of course, we, ah, everyone is wondering what, ah, hoping you will be able to stay in your lovely home here . . ."

Rosalind wished she could say what she thought about the woman's transparent inquiry about their lovely house, selfish harridan that she was. She kept her mouth shut.

Henrietta reached over to pat Rosalind's hand. "It must be so very difficult for you, dear, what with all your years as Bath's most eligible young lady, superior in wealth, and, of course, looks as well. I daresay you will find your life quite different now. But that is not for me to say, though everyone is speaking of how sad they feel for you.

"And so," Henrietta went on, "I said to Lady Melrose, I said, I was quite sure you would not avoid the Pump Room tomorrow because . . ."

Jaspers announced Mrs. Winslough and Lady Fleming. Mrs. Winslough came directly to Rosalind and clasped her to her broad bosom. "My dearest girl, we are devastated, simply horrified to hear of your reversals."

Rosalind gently disengaged herself. "Thank you for your concern."

"Oh, you are so brave, so gracious, Miss Rosalind, I so admire your composure."

"Yes," Henrietta said, assuming control of the conversation, "Miss Elliott is brave in the face of misfortune. But of course she still has her Fosswell Manor. None of us should consider her destitute. Correct, Rosalind?"

She nodded.

Henrietta leaned forward and spoke in conspiratorial tones. "I was finally able to persuade Admiral Gladfeller to tell us about Philip's exploits at sea. He does not talk of it himself, not even to his father, but the admiral enlightened us. Philip is much too modest to admit it, but he is quite the hero. He fought in many battles, you know, and never lost a major encounter, the admiral said."

Rosalind exchanged an amused glance with Lady Rotherford. Their new problem would be getting rid of all the callers in time for Grandmother's nap.

* * *

Captain Chadwell strolled toward Rosalind after Sunday services at the Abbey. "Good day, Miss Elliott."

He gave that crooked smile that made her heart dance. "Captain Chadwell, it is good to see you."

They moved a few steps away from the crowds gathered in the Yard.

"I can hardly believe the change in people," he said. "I have been invited to become a member of several clubs and to join the informal gatherings at Lord Cantillon's, where there is said to be gaming every night. I've been offered an interest in a race-horse and at least ten merchants have left their cards welcoming my custom."

Rosalind raised her eyebrows. "Meaning a wealthy man is expected to part with his money in a wide variety of ways, I believe."

For the past week, she had seen him infrequently, as they allowed the twin stories of financial disaster and heroic reward to circulate. Rosalind was impatient to be alone with him again and know the warmth of his arms and the exquisite touch of his lips.

Philip chuckled. "I have heard the most amazing stories about myself. I own a vast estate near Lymington, practically half the New Forest, you know. And that is not nearly as fantastic as the rumor I have extensive interests in Lancashire coal mines. But everywhere I go, I hear such praise of your courage, Miss Elliott."

"Yes, I have noticed how talk of my bravery is an efficient way to say even more about my losses, which, you may be interested to hear, now include an entire network of banks all over the West Country."

"Amazing. But, Rosalind, how much longer must this go on?"

She gazed up into his eyes and felt her heart race faster. "We said we would wait at least a month."

He did not move a muscle for what seemed an eternity. "Rosalind, you have been a top-notch leader of this campaign. But I think it is time for a change of command. I have exercised all the patience in my arsenal."

"Captain Chadwell, you may take command, but I yield to no one when it comes to impatience."

He put his arms around her. "I propose to see the archbishop today and secure a license. We can be wed this week without waiting for the banns."

She closed her eyes and leaned against him. "Nothing would please me more."

He drew away and smiled down at her. "You make me the happiest of men, Rosalind."

"We must tell Grandmother and Lady Isiline. And your father."

"I imagine they know exactly what is going on. They are standing over there watching us."

She gasped, suddenly realizing where they stood. The Abbey Yard was dotted with people, all staring in their direction. "Why everyone in Bath is watching!"

Before he let her go, he placed a quick kiss on the tip of her nose. "A suitable addendum to the current commentaries, my dearest almost-wife."

Historical Romance from
Jo Ann Ferguson

__**Christmas Bride**	0-8217-6760-7	**$4.99US/$6.99CAN**
__**His Lady Midnight**	0-8217-6863-8	**$4.99US/$6.99CAN**
__**A Guardian's Angel**	0-8217-7174-4	**$4.99US/$6.99CAN**
__**His Unexpected Bride**	0-8217-7175-2	**$4.99US/$6.99CAN**
__**A Sister's Quest**	0-8217-6788-7	**$5.50US/$7.50CAN**
__**Moonlight on Water**	0-8217-7310-0	**$5.99US/$7.99CAN**

Put a Little Romance in Your Life With
Melanie George

__**Devil May Care**
   0-8217-7008-X $5.99US/$7.99CAN

__**Handsome Devil**
   0-8217-7009-8   5.99US/$7.99CAN

__**Devil's Due**
   0-8217-7010-1 $5.99US/$7.99CAN

__**The Mating Game**
   0-8217-7120-5 $5.99US/$7.99CAN